ZADIG/L'INGÉNU

ADVISORY EDITOR: BETTY RADICE

François-Marie Arouet (1694–1778), who later took the name of Voltaire, was the son of a notary, and educated at a Jesuit school in Paris. Although his father wished him to study law, he determined on a literary career. Gaining an introduction to the intellectual life of Paris, he soon won a not altogether enviable reputation as a writer of satires and odes, for the suspicion of having written a satire on the Regent resulted in six months' imprisonment in the Bastille. On his release, his first tragedy, *Oedipe*, was performed (1718) in Paris with great success; and soon after he published a national epic poem he had written in prison, *La Henriade* (1724), which placed him with Homer and Virgil in the eyes of his contemporaries. After a second term of imprisonment in the Bastille, Voltaire spent the years 1726–9 in England, and returned to France full of enthusiasm for the intellectual activity and the more tolerant form of government he had found there. His enthusiasm and his indictment of the French system of government are expressed in his *Philosophic Letters* (1733), whose sale was forbidden in France. The next fifteen years were spent at the country seat of his friend, Madame du Châtelet, where he wrote his most popular tragedies and *Zadig*, a witty Eastern tale, and started work on his *Century of Louis XIV*. After Madame du Châtelet's death in 1749, Voltaire visited the court of Frederick the Great, and while there completed his historical work, *Essay on Customs (Essai sur les Moeurs et l'Esprit des Nations)*, and began his *Philosophic Dictionary*, but he and Frederick did not agree for long, and in 1753 he left Prussia. France was still unsafe, and after two years' wandering he settled in Geneva. During his last, most brilliant, twenty years, he wrote *Candide*, his dialogues, and more tales, and published his *Philosophical Dictionary* (1764) in 'pocket' form, while conducting a ceaseless attack on what he called the 'infamous thing', i.e. all manifestations of tyranny and persecution by a privileged orthodoxy in Church and State. He died aged eighty-four after a triumphant visit to Paris from which he had been exiled for so long.

John Butt was born in 1906 and educated at Shrewsbury and Merton College, Oxford, where he read English. Until his death in 1965, he was Regius Professor of Rhetoric and English Literature at Edinburgh, and he also worked at the Universities of London and Newcastle, and in America. Much of his life was devoted to the Twickenham edition of the poems of Alexander Pope. His translation of Voltaire's *Candide* is published in Penguin Classics.

VOLTAIRE

ZADIG · L'INGÉNU

TRANSLATED
WITH AN INTRODUCTION
BY JOHN BUTT

PENGUIN BOOKS

PENGUIN BOOKS

Published by the Penguin Group
Penguin Books Ltd, 80 Strand, London WC2R 0RL, England
Penguin Putnam Inc., 375 Hudson Street, New York, New York 10014, USA
Penguin Books Australia Ltd, 250 Camberwell Road, Camberwell, Victoria 3124, Australia
Penguin Books Canada Ltd, 10 Alcorn Avenue, Toronto, Ontario, Canada M4V 3B2
Penguin Books India (P) Ltd, 11 Community Centre, Panchsheel Park, New Delhi – 110 017, India
Penguin Books (NZ) Ltd, Cnr Rosedale and Airborne Roads, Albany, Auckland, New Zealand
Penguin Books (South Africa) (Pty) Ltd, 24 Sturdee Avenue, Rosebank 2196, South Africa

Penguin Books Ltd, Registered Offices: 80 Strand, London WC2R 0RL, England

www.penguin.com

First published 1964

034

Copyright © John Butt, 1964
All rights reserved

Printed and bound in Great Britain by Clays Ltd, Elcograf S.p.A.
Set in Linotype Granjon

www.greenpenguin.co.uk

CONTENTS

ZADIG

L'INGÉNU
(THE CHILD OF NATURE)

INTRODUCTION

READERS of these two tales who are already acquainted with *Candide* will find themselves exploring familiar territory. They will immediately recognize the wit and buffoonery and the power of invention to which *Candide* has introduced them; the adventures are as numerous and as neatly told; and Fortune behaves as outrageously as ever, while man receives both her buffets and her blessings with his customary resilience. But though all three stories are clearly the work of one mind, they exhibit such differences as might be expected from the development of that mind over a period of twenty years. *Zadig, or Destiny, an Oriental Tale*, though one of the earliest of Voltaire's tales (1747), is the work of an experienced man of letters who had already lived more than half his life. An Eastern tale had an irresistible appeal to the first generation that succumbed to the charms of *The Arabian Nights*, after their translation into French between 1704 and 1717. From that time onward, both in France and England, writers had suffered their imaginations to dwell upon the Near East, a vast tract of country which differed from the west as a setting for a story in that riches could be more opulently displayed, power more imperially exercised, and sages or hermits more frequently discovered and more patiently attended to. These stories, however exotic their setting, and however fantastic their detail, offered opportunities of reflection upon experiences common to all men. A year or two after the publication of *Zadig*, Dr Johnson was writing a number of Eastern tales for publication in his periodical, *The Rambler*; one teaches the vanity of idle hopes, another of sensual gratification, another of expecting the reward of benevolence. Voltaire's imagination was more volatile than Johnson's; his stories sparkle more brightly with wit and

7

absurdity; but no less than Johnson's, his moral is explicit, and the separate episodes of Zadig's career are like so many unrelated stories in the Englishman's periodical essays. If the episodes have a connexion other than a protagonist common to them all, it lies in the respect that a well-educated, well-balanced mind deserves, in the triumph of good sense allied to good behaviour. Zadig owes his first success (in Chapter 3) to skill in interpreting evidence such as Sherlock Holmes would have admired, but he maintains it (through the next four chapters) by his wisdom, his discretion, and his gentle behaviour. In subsequent episodes, he is often the victim of passion and prejudice in high estate, and he has to contend with the most varied forms of stupid, irrational behaviour in those he meets; but good sense, patience in persuasion, ingenuity, and courage ensure his eventual triumph.

A man can scarcely avoid suffering in a world like this, though if he is endowed with enough sense and sensibility he will succeed in making his way. That seems to have been Voltaire's belief. But need the world have been organized so badly? If the Creator is good, how is it he allows so much to happen that no sensitive and sensible man can possibly approve? The problem was an old one, but it had recently been discussed with new enthusiasm. Voltaire had read and admired Pope's *Essay on Man*. In that poem Pope had counselled a patient optimism: as men, we have not the range of vision to see how a present evil is compensated by a future good, or how each event contributes to the great design that God alone can comprehend. *Zadig* shows Voltaire pondering this answer. The consequences of his actions are always concealed from Zadig; but when the event is over he rarely fails to reflect on the bewildering ways of fate. 'Think of it! Eighty ounces of gold as a forfeit for not noticing a little bitch! Condemned to be beheaded for four bad verses in praise of the King! Nearly strangled because the Queen had some slippers the colour of my cap! Reduced to slavery for having rescued a woman from a beating, and within an inch of being burned at the stake for having saved the lives of all the young widows in Arabia!'

It is not until the penultimate chapter that Voltaire attempts to grapple with the theological aspect of the problem. There Zadig meets the Angel Jesrad disguised as a hermit, and the two set out together on a journey. The hermit behaves more and more outrageously as he rewards good with evil and evil with good. At last he throws off his disguise and justifies his actions. Zadig is reluctant to accept his explanations: 'but wouldn't it have been better . . . but must there always be crime and misfortune ... but supposing there were no evil ...?' To all these questions the Angel gives the official answer, the answer of the *Essay on Man*. He speaks with energy and authority, yet it is Zadig who has the last word: ' "But" – said he. As he said the word the Angel took flight towards the Empyrean, and Zadig fell on his knees, worshipping providence in true submissiveness.' An ambiguous conclusion? Perhaps; but this quizzical dissatisfaction with the official doctrine was to give way to a counterblast in *Candide*, published twelve years later.

In *Zadig* and *Candide*, the comic view prevails. Men and women suffer, but they are never down for long. Virtue and good sense support them, and hope encourages them. But *The Child of Nature* (*L'Ingénu*), the latest of these stories, is more sombre. The opening chapters, in which the Child of Nature, bred up amongst the Huron Indians, returns accidentally to his father's home in Lower Brittany, are as gay and irreverent as the two earlier tales have led us to expect. Voltaire was not only amusing himself at the expense of the obstinate, bigoted, and kindly Breton provincials, but he was giving a wider circle of readers the opportunity of seeing themselves as others saw them. Addison had played the same game in the *Spectator* (No. 50), twelve months after Queen Anne had given audience to four Iroquois kings in April 1710. One of these Red Indian chieftains was supposed to have left behind in his lodgings a little bundle of papers in which he had recorded some impressions of his visit. Amongst some 'wild remarks' the *Spectator* noticed that 'there now and then appears something very reasonable': Equally reasonable are the Child of Nature's comments on the customs of the land he was visiting; and just as Addison's chieftain had difficulty in accepting a tradition that St Paul's Cathedral 'was designed for men to pay their devotions in', though there were 'several reasons which make us think that the natives of this country had formerly among them some sort of worship', so the Huron was perplexed by the differences between religious practice as it is described in the Bible and the ceremonies of the modern church.

But the Child of Nature is not some Noble Savage held up for admiration. The way of a man with a maid in Huronia, for example, is not to be imitated over here. The Huron's sensibilities are keen, his reason untrammelled by the nonsense and the prejudice instilled into us in childhood; but he still needs educating, and this was the opportunity which imprisonment with the worthy Jansenist provided. He was being given time for reading and reflexion; and like a hardy tree, he spread out roots and branches as soon as he was transplanted to a favourable soil (p. 152). Far from offering a romantic plea for education by Nature, Voltaire was at pains to emphasize the educative importance of cultivated society.

The Child of Nature's education is completed by suffering. Not only is he imprisoned without good cause and detained without trial, but his release is procured by means that lead to the death of his darling, the lovely St Yves. When Voltaire came to write *L'Ingénu*, he was fresh from his work in procuring posthumous justice for Jean Calas, the protestant merchant who had been put to death by torture on a charge of having murdered a son who had adopted the Roman Catholic faith. This was only the most famous of several causes in which Voltaire appealed for a spirit of toleration and championed the victims of privilege; and the second half of *L'Ingénu* bears ample witness to his detestation of the insolence, indifference, and injustice of those who wielded power in church and state.

But besides reflecting the campaign that Voltaire had been waging against the forces of oppression, this tale seems also to mark a further stage in his attempt to understand the problem of evil. Suffering has added another dimension to the characters of the lovely St Yves and the Huron; at the end of the tale they are less naïve, and the Huron in particular shows more balance, more depth, and more discernment. We like them better for what they have gone through; whereas our feelings towards Zadig and Candide, like the characters themselves, are largely unaffected by their experiences. This can be attributed to the difference between a comic and a tragic interpretation of life, for tragedy lends itself more readily than comedy to sympathetic development within a character. But in showing how human character can be developed by suffering, Voltaire is surely making a more mature contribution to the problem of evil than those he had offered in *Zadig* and *Candide*, one which though less vivacious is more satisfying in the end.

The texts upon which the translations have been based are those of Verdun L. Saulnier for *Zadig*, and of William R. Jones for *L'Ingénu*, both published by the Librairie Droz (Geneva) and the Librairie Minard (Paris). These editions are themselves based upon the edition published by Cramer (Geneva, 1756), which preserves the final revisions for which Voltaire can certainly be held responsible. In the posthumous Kehl edition of 1785 two chapters are inserted in *Zadig* after Chapter 13, entitled 'La Danse' and 'Les Yeux Bleus'. They may be authentic, but I have followed Professor Saulnier in rejecting them. From these two editions I have derived much help; I am also deeply indebted for assistance at several points to my sister-in-law, Mrs Ruth Butt, and to my colleague, Dr Joanna Kitchin, and for practical support and encouragement from start to finish to my wife.

J.B.

BIOGRAPHICAL NOTE

FRANÇOISE-MARIE AROUET (1694-1778), who later took the name of Voltaire, was the son of a notary and educated at a Jesuit school in Paris. His father wanted him to study the law, but the young man was determined on a literary career. He gained an introduction to the intellectual life of Paris, and soon won a reputation as a writer of satires and odes – a not altogether enviable reputation, for the suspicion of having written a satire on the Regent procured him a term of six months' imprisonment in the Bastille. On his release, his first tragedy, *Œdipe*, was performed (1718) in Paris with great success; and soon after he published the poem he had written in prison, a national epic, *La Henriade* (1724), which placed him with Homer and Virgil in the eyes of his contemporaries.

After a second term of imprisonment in the Bastille, Voltaire spent three years (1726–9) in England, and returned to France full of enthusiasm for the intellectual activity and the more tolerant form of government he found in this country. His enthusiasm and his indictment of the French system of government are expressed in his *Philosophic Letters* (1733), whose sale was absolutely forbidden in France.

The next fifteen years were spent at the country seat of his friend, Madame du Châtelet, where he wrote *Zadig* and his most popular tragedies, and started work on his *Century of Louis XIV*.

After Mme du Châtelet's death in 1749, Voltaire was induced to pay a prolonged visit to the Court of Frederick the Great, with whom he had been in correspondence for several years. While there he completed his important historical work *Essay on Customs* (*Essai sur les mœurs et l'esprit des nations*), and began his *Philosophic Dictionary*. Voltaire and Frederick could not agree for long, and in 1753 Voltaire decided to leave Prussia. But he was not safe in France. After two years of wandering, he settled near Geneva, and at last made a home at Ferney.

It was during these last, and most brilliant, twenty years of his life that he wrote *Candide*, his dialogues, and more tales, including *L'Ingénu*, and published his widely-read *Philosophic Dictionary* (1764) in 'pocket' form, while conducting his ceaseless and energetic attack against what he called the 'infamous thing' – that is to say, all manifestations of tyranny and persecution by a privileged orthodoxy in church and state.

He died at the age of eighty-four, after a triumphant visit to the Paris from which he had been exiled for so long.

ZADIG

OR

DESTINY

AN ORIENTAL TALE

IMPRIMATUR

I THE undersigned, who claim to be a scholar, and even a wit, have read this manuscript. I have to admit that I have found it curious, amusing, moral, philosophical, and likely to please even those who hate novels. I have therefore damned it, and have assured the Lord Chief Justice that it is a detestable performance.

*The eighteenth day of the month Schewal,
in the year 837 of the Hejira*

ENCHANTER of Eyes, Disturber of Hearts, Light of the Mind, I kiss not the dust from your feet, because you rarely walk, or walk only upon Iranian carpets or on roses. I present to you the translation of a book written by a Wise Man of old, whose good fortune it was to have nothing else to do but occupy himself in writing the story of Zadig, a work which has more to tell than meets the eye.

I beg you to read and consider it; for though you are in the springtime of life, though all pleasures are at your command, though you are beautiful, and though your talents enhance your beauty; though you are praised from sunset to sunrise, and therefore by rights you should have no common sense; yet you have a good understanding and a refined taste, and I have heard you argue better than the old Dervishes with their long beards and tasselled caps. You are discreet, yet not distrustful; you are sweet-tempered, without being weak; you discriminate in your charities; you love your friends, and you never make enemies. Your wit never borrows charms from slander; you say no harm and do no harm, though both are so much in your power. In short your soul has always seemed to me as spotless as your beauty. Besides, you possess a little stock of philosophy, which makes me think that this wise man's work will appeal to you more than to any other lady.

It was written originally in the ancient Chaldean tongue, which neither of us understands. It was then translated into Arabic, to entertain the famous Sultan Oulougbeg, at about the time when the Arabs and the Persians were beginning to write the Thousand and One Nights, and the Thousand and One Days, and so forth. Ouloug preferred reading *Zadig*; but the Sultanas enjoyed the Arabian Nights much more. 'How can you prefer stories,' asked the wise Ouloug, 'which have neither sense nor reason?' 'But that is just why we do like them,' replied the Sultanas.

I am sure that you will not resemble them, but will prove instead a true Ouloug. I even hope, when you grow tired of general conversation – which is like the Arabian Nights, except that it is less amusing – that I may have the honour of a moment's rational discourse with you. If you had been Thalestris in the time of Alexander son of Philip, or the Queen of Sheba in the time of Solomon, those would have been the kings who would have visited you.

I implore the Heavenly Powers that your pleasures be unalloyed, your beauty lasting, and your good fortune without end.

SADI

CHAPTER I

*

BLIND IN ONE EYE

THERE lived at Babylon in the time of King Moabdar a young man called Zadig, whose amiable character had been improved by a good education. Though he was both rich and young, he knew how to control his passions. He was not in the least pretentious; he did not wish to be always in the right, and he could respect the weakness of his fellow men. Though amply endowed with wit, it was remarkable that he never jeered at the vague, inconsequential, noisy tittle-tattle, the bold slanders, the ignorant assertions, the blatant puns, and the empty noise of words which in Babylon passed for conversation. He had learned from the first book of Zoroaster that self-esteem is a balloon blown up with wind which will let loose a storm when it is punctured. Even more commendable was his attitude to women, for he never pretended to scorn them and never boasted of his conquests. He was openhanded as well, and was never afraid of befriending where he looked for no return, since he followed the precept of Zoroaster: *'When you feed, feed the dogs also, even though they bite you.'* To all these qualities was added a good measure of wisdom, for he made it his practice to consort with the wise. He had been instructed in the learning of the ancient Chaldees, and understood as much as was known about natural causes at that time; he also knew as much metaphysics as has ever been known, and that is precious little. He was firmly persuaded, in spite of the latest philosophy, that the year consists of three hundred and sixty-five days and a quarter, and that the sun is the centre of the universe; and when the chief mages arrogantly told him that he harboured dangerous opinions, that it was contrary to the national interest to believe that the sun revolved on its own axis, and that there were twelve months in the year, he held his peace and refused to be moved.

As Zadig was wealthy, he had no lack of friends; and as he was also blessed with good health, a pleasing appearance, a sprightly well-governed wit, and a generous heart, he felt assured of happiness. He was engaged to be married to Semira, whose beauty, birth, and fortune made her the best match in Babylon. He felt for her a solid and virtuous attachment, and Semira was passionately devoted to him.

One day shortly before their wedding they were taking a walk near one of the gates of Babylon, under the beautiful palm trees which line the banks of the river Euphrates, when they saw some men approaching them armed with swords and arrows. They were the retainers of young Orcan, the chief minister's nephew, who had been led to believe by his uncle's parasites that he could do what he liked. He had neither Zadig's graces nor his virtues, but he thought he was the better man of the two and was tormented at not being preferred. This fit of jealousy was occasioned by his vanity, and made him think that he loved Semira to distraction. He therefore resolved to kidnap her. While carrying her off, his minions were so brutal as to wound her and to shed the blood of one whose appearance would have softened a Bengal tiger. The heavens were rent with her screams. 'My dearest,' she cried, 'they are tearing me away from the man I most adore.' She took no heed for her own danger: all she thought of was her dear Zadig. He rushed to her defence with all the ardour which love and valour bestow. With no help but what his two slaves could give, he put the ravishers to flight, and carried Semira home fainting and bleeding. When she opened her eyes, she saw who it was who had rescued her and said:

'Oh, Zadig! Once I loved you as my future husband. Now I love you as one to whom I owe my honour and my life.'

Never was heart so affected as Semira's. Never did such charming lips express more tender feelings. Never did words

convey such warmth of gratitude or ardour of such unques-
tionable propriety.

Her injury was slight and she soon recovered; but Zadig
had been more seriously hurt. An arrow had struck him close
to his eye and had made a deep wound. Semira prayed
without ceasing for her lover's recovery. Night and day the
tears streamed from her eyes, as she awaited the moment
when Zadig could revel in her glances; but an abscess
developed in the wounded eye which caused the gravest concern. A letter was sent to Memphis to summon a celebrated
doctor called Hermes, who arrived with a large retinue. He
examined the patient, and announced that he would lose his
eye; he even predicted the day and hour when this deplorable
event would take place.

'If it had been the right eye', said he, 'I could have healed
it. But wounds in the left eye are incurable.'

The people of Babylon were sorry about poor Zadig's fate,
but they were greatly impressed by Dr Hermes's learning.
Two days later the abscess burst, and Zadig completely recovered. Hermes thereupon wrote a book in which he proved
that Zadig had no business to recover. Zadig did not read a
word of it; but as soon as he could go out, he decided to pay a
visit to her in whom his future happiness lay, and for whom
alone he treasured his sight.

Semira had been in the country for the last three days. He
learned on the way to her house that that beautiful lady had
openly declared her unconquerable aversion to one-eyed men,
and had just married Orcan that very evening. On hearing
the news, he fainted. Grief brought him to the very edge of
the grave and he suffered a long illness. But in the end,
reason triumphed over his affliction, and the cruelty which
he had experienced even served to console him.

'I have suffered so bitterly from the caprice of a girl brought
up at Court,' said he, 'that I must now find a wife in the
city.'

His choice fell upon Azora, a young lady of good birth and

sound understanding. He married her, and enjoyed the sweets of the tenderest passion for a whole month. He merely noticed that she was somewhat frivolous and much disposed to find in the most handsome young men the fullest endowment of wit and virtue.

*

CHAPTER 2

THE NOSE

ONE day Azora came home from a walk in great indignation.

'What is the matter, my dear?' asked Zadig. 'What can
have thrown you into such a temper?'

'You would have been as indignant yourself,' she replied,
'if you had seen what I have just witnessed. I went to condole
with Cosrou's young widow, who two days ago had a tomb
made for her young husband near the stream which flows
beside the meadow. In her grief she vowed to the Gods that
she would remain at the tomb as long as the stream ran by.'

'Well,' said Zadig, 'what an admirable woman she must be,
and how faithfully she must have loved her husband!'

'Ah!' replied Azora, 'but if you knew what she was doing
when I went to see her!'

'Well, Azora, my dear, what was it?'

'She was diverting the stream.'

Azora then launched into a long tirade, and uttered violent
reproaches against the young widow, a display of virtue at
which Zadig was not at all pleased.

He had a friend called Cador, a young person in whom
his wife discovered more honesty and worth than in others.
He took him into his confidence, and assured himself of his
co-operation, as best he could, by a handsome present. Azora
went to spend a couple of days with one of her friends in
the country. When she returned home on the third day, her
weeping servants informed her that her husband had died
suddenly the very night she left, that no one had dared to
bring her this melancholy news, and that Zadig had just been
buried in the tomb of his fathers at the bottom of the garden.

Azora wept and tore her hair, and swore that she would die too. That evening Cador begged leave to speak to her, and they both sat weeping together. Next day they wept less and dined alone in each other's company. Cador confided to her that his friend had left him the greater part of his estate, and that he would be happy to share his fortune with her. The lady was angry and shed some tears, but at length she grew composed. Supper lasted longer than dinner, and they began to talk with less restraint: Azora spoke in praise of the deceased, but admitted that he had some faults from which Cador was free.

In the middle of supper Cador complained of a violent pain in his spleen. The lady expressed alarm and earnestly bade her servants to bring all the essences from her dressing-table to see whether any of them was good for a pain in the spleen. She said how sorry she was that the great Dr Hermes was no longer in Babylon, and she even went so far as to touch the place where it hurt Cador so severely.

'Are you subject to these cruel attacks?' she asked tenderly.

'They sometimes bring me to the edge of the grave,' he replied, 'and there is only one remedy which brings me any relief; that is, to apply to my side a dead man's nose.'

'What a strange remedy!' said Azora.

'No stranger,' he replied, 'than the bags which Dr Arnou prescribes for apoplexy.' *

This answer, together with the young man's exceptional merit, confirmed the lady in her decision.

'After all,' she reflected, 'when my husband passes over the bridge of Chinavar from this world to the next, will the Angel Asrael be less ready to admit him because his nose is not quite so long in the second life as in the first?'

She therefore took a razor and went to her husband's tomb. There she shed some tears before approaching to cut

* There was at that time a Babylonian called Arnou, who according to the newspapers cured and prevented all apoplexies with a bag hung from the patient's neck. [Voltaire's note.]

off the nose from Zadig's body, which she found laid out in
the grave. Zadig got up, holding his nose with one hand and
seizing the razor with the other.

'Madam,' said he, 'no more exclamations at young Madam
Cosrou's behaviour. Cutting off my nose is just as bad as
diverting a stream.'

CHAPTER 3

*

THE DOG AND THE HORSE

ZADIG found, as it is written in the Book of Zend, that the first month of marriage is the Honeymoon and the second is the Wormwoodmoon. It was not long before he was obliged to divorce Azora, who had become too difficult to live with, and he decided to seek consolation in the study of Nature.

'There is no greater happiness,' said he, 'than that which a philosopher enjoys in reading the great book which God has set before our eyes. The truths he there discovers become his own. He feasts his spirit with lofty thoughts. He lives a life of tranquillity, in which no man gives him cause for fear and and no loving wife comes to cut off his nose.'

Full of these ideas, he retired to a country seat on the banks of the Euphrates. He did not spend his time there in calculating how many inches of water flowed each second under the arches of a bridge, or whether the signs of the Zodiac affect the rainfall: whether the month of the mouse, for instance, is wetter than the month of the sheep. He did not speculate on how to make silk from spiders' webs, or china from broken bottles; but he did study the properties of animals and plants, and soon learned to recognize subtle differences which others failed to discern.

One day as he was walking near a little wood he saw one of the Queen's eunuchs running towards him, followed by several Officers of the Guard who seemed to be in great anxiety. They were rushing hither and thither like men distracted, looking for some precious object which they had lost.

'Young man,' said the chief eunuch to Zadig, 'have you seen the Queen's dog anywhere?'

'It is a bitch, not a dog,' replied Zadig, modestly.

'Yes, you're right,' said the chief eunuch.

'It is a little Spaniel bitch,' Zadig went on. 'She has recently had puppies, she limps in the left foreleg, and her ears are very long.'

'Then you have seen her,' said the chief eunuch, quite out of breath.

'No,' replied Zadig. 'I have never seen her. I never even knew that the Queen had a bitch.'

At that very moment, by one of the customary freaks of fortune, the finest horse in the King's stable had escaped from the hands of its groom on the plains of Babylon. The chief huntsman and all the remaining officers were running after it in as much anxiety as the chief eunuch had shown for the bitch. The chief huntsman went up to Zadig and asked him if he had seen the King's horse go by.

'There isn't a better galloper,' replied Zadig. 'It is five foot high, with remarkably small hooves, and a tail three and a half feet long. The bosses on its bit are of twenty-three carat gold, and it is shod with silver of eleven deniers proof.'

'Which way did it go? Where is it?' asked the chief huntsman.

'I have not seen it,' replied Zadig. 'This is the first I've heard of it.'

The chief huntsman and the chief eunuch were in no doubt that Zadig had stolen the King's horse and the Queen's bitch. They had him brought before the Lord Treasurer's court, who sentenced him to be flogged and to spend the rest of his days in Siberia. The sentence was scarcely passed when the horse and the bitch were found. The judges were therefore in the painful position of having to alter their decision; but they sentenced Zadig to pay four hundred ounces of gold for having declared that he had not seen what he had seen. The fine had first to be paid, but Zadig was afterwards allowed to plead his cause before the Lord Treasurer's Council. He spoke as follows:

'Luminaries of Justice! Unfathomable Depths of Knowledge! Mirrors of Truth, who possess the weight of lead, the strength of iron, the brilliance of diamonds, and a close resemblance to gold! Being granted permission to speak before this august assembly, I swear to you by Ormuzd that I have never seen the Queen's most honourable bitch nor the sacred horse belonging to the King of Kings. This is what happened. I was taking a walk near the coppice where I afterwards met the most reverend eunuch and the most illustrious chief huntsman. I noticed the tracks of an animal in the sandy soil, which I readily took to be those of a little dog. Some long but delicate furrows, traced in the sand wherever it was raised between the prints of the paws, showed me that it was a bitch with hanging dugs, which must therefore have had puppies a few days before. Other tracks of a different kind, which always appeared to have brushed the sand at either side of the forefeet, showed me that its ears were very long; and as I noticed that the sand was always more deeply impressed by one paw than by the other three, I concluded that our august Queen's little bitch was a trifle lame, if I may dare to say so.

'As for the horse which belongs to the King of Kings, you must know that as I was walking along the paths of this wood, I noticed some horseshoe prints all at equal distances. "There's a horse with a fine gallop," I said to myself. In a straight stretch of path only seven feet wide, the dust had been lightly brushed from the trees on both sides at a distance of three and a half feet from the centre of the path. "This horse," said I, "has a tail three and a half feet long, which must have swept off the dust on both sides as it waved." The trees formed an arcade five feet high. When I noticed that some of the leaves were newly fallen, I deduced that the horse must have touched them, and that he was therefore five feet high also. As for the bit, it must be made of twenty-three carat gold, because the horse had rubbed the bosses against a stone which I knew to be touchstone, and which I therefore tested. And finally I judged from the marks which the horseshoes had left on a different kind of stone that it was shod with silver of eleven deniers proof.'

The assembled judges admired Zadig's deep and subtle penetration. The news of it even reached the King and Queen. In the antechambers, in the drawing room, and in the council chamber no one talked of anything but Zadig; and though several mages considered that he should be burnt as a sorcerer, the King commanded the fine of four hundred ounces of gold to which he had been sentenced to be repaid to him. The Clerk of the Court, the Gentlemen Ushers, and the Procurators Fiscal visited him in great state to repay the four hundred ounces. They retained a mere three hundred and ninety-eight of them for legal expenses, and their servants had to be tipped.

Zadig saw how dangerous it sometimes is to be too clever, and he determined on the next occasion to say nothing of what he had seen.

The occasion soon arrived. A prisoner of state escaped, and passed by Zadig's window. Zadig was questioned and made no reply. But he was proved to have been looking out of his window, and was condemned for this crime to pay five hundred ounces of gold. He thanked the judges for their clemency, as the custom is in Babylon.

'Good Heavens,' he said to himself. 'What trouble a man can get into if he takes a walk in a wood after the Queen's bitch and the King's horse have passed by! How dangerous it is to sit at a window, and how difficult to be happy in this life!'

CHAPTER 4

*

GREEN EYES

ZADIG decided to seek consolation for the buffets of fortune in philosophy and friendship. He owned an elegant house on the outskirts of Babylon, and there he gathered together the choicest products of art, and all the pleasures in which a gentleman might indulge. In the morning his library was open to scholars, and in the evening he welcomed to his table the best society in Babylon. But he soon learned what dangerous men scholars are. A great controversy arose about one of the laws of Zoroaster, which forbids the eating of griffins. Why proscribe the griffin, said one party, if the creature does not exist? But it must exist, said the rest, since Zoroaster does not wish it to be eaten! Zadig determined to reconcile the two parties, so he said:

'If griffins do exist, we mustn't eat them. If they don't, we certainly can't eat them. Thus either way we shall obey Zoroaster.'

One scholar, who had written thirteen volumes on the properties of the griffin, and who was an important theologian as well, hastened to report Zadig to an Archimage called Yebor, who, besides being the most stupid of the Chaldeans, was also the most fanatical. This man would have had Zadig brought to the stake for the greater glory of the Sun, while he intoned with relish appropriate passages from the liturgy of Zoroaster. Zadig's friend Cador – a friend is worth more than a hundred priests – called upon Yebor, and said to the old man:

'Long live the Sun and the griffins; but think twice before you punish Zadig. He is a saint. He keeps griffins in his courtyard and does not eat them; his accuser is a heretic, who is so bold as to maintain that rabbits have cloven feet and are not unclean!'

'In that case,' said Yebor, shaking his bald head, 'Zadig must be brought to the stake for dangerous thoughts on griffins, and the other man for slander on rabbits.'

Cador hushed the matter up with the help of one of the maids of honour by whom he had had a child and who had great influence in the College of Mages. No one was brought to the stake, at which several of the Reverend Doctors murmured and predicted the downfall of Babylon; but Zadig exclaimed:

'On what does happiness depend! I am at the mercy of everything in this world, even of creatures which don't exist!'

He cursed the whole tribe of scholars and decided to live only in high society.

He invited to his house the most worthy men and the most agreeable ladies in Babylon. His supper parties, which were often preceded by a concert, were extremely elegant and were enlivened by delightful talk. He had managed to prohibit any parade of wit at his table, for that is the surest way of missing the mark and of spoiling the most brilliant conversation. Vanity played no part in his choice of friends or of food, for in everything he preferred solid worth to mere show. That was how he earned real respect, though he never aspired to it.

Opposite his house there lived a certain Arimazes, whose coarse features betrayed a wicked disposition. He was consumed with rancour and puffed up with pride; but what was worst of all, he was an insufferable bore. Because he had had no success in society, he took his revenge by railing at it. Rich as he was, there were few toadies who would sit at his table. The sound of carriages entering Zadig's drive of an evening was a source of irritation to him, and the sound of Zadig's praises annoyed him even more. He sometimes went to Zadig's parties and sat down to table uninvited: on such occasions he spoiled the mirth of the company as the Harpies are said to have tainted the food they touched. On one occasion he decided to give a party in honour of a certain lady; but she, instead of accepting his invitation, went to have supper with Zadig. On another occasion when he and Zadig were talking together in the Palace, a Minister came up and invited Zadig to supper but did not include Arimazes. The most bitter hatred often has no greater foundation. Arimazes, whose nickname in Babylon was Green Eyes, determined to ruin Zadig, because he was called Zadig the Happy. Opportunities for making mischief are found a hundred times a day, but the chance of doing a good turn comes but once a year; so it is written in the book of Zoroaster.

Green Eyes went to call upon Zadig, whom he found walking in his garden with two friends and a lady, making gallant remarks to them simply for the pleasure that it gave him. The conversation turned upon the war against the vassal Prince of Hyrcania, which the King had just brought to a happy conclusion. Zadig, who had distinguished himself in the campaign, gave high praise to the King, and even higher to the lady. Taking a notebook from his pocket, he wrote on it four lines of verse which he had composed on the spot, and handed it to his beautiful guest to read. His friends begged him to allow them to see the verses; but modesty, or rather self-respect, forbade. He knew, of course, that impromptu verses have no value except for those in whose honour they are written. He tore in half the leaf of the notebook on which he had been writing, and threw the two pieces into a large rosebush where it was useless to look for them. Just then a shower of rain drove the company back to the house. Green Eyes stayed behind in the garden, and searched until he discovered one piece of the paper. It had been so torn that each half line of verse made sense, and even scanned; but by a still stranger chance these half lines formed a quatrain which greatly libelled the King. It read as follows:

By most abandoned riot
Confirmed upon the throne,
In times of public quiet
He is the foe alone.

Green Eyes was happy for the first time in his life. He held in his hand something to ruin an upright and popular man. Exulting in his cruel triumph, he sent the lampoon, written in Zadig's hand, to the King himself; and Zadig, his two friends, and the lady were all thrown into prison. The case was soon over without being properly heard. When Zadig was summoned to receive his sentence, Green Eyes accosted him and taunted him with writing bad verses. Zadig did not pride himself on being a good poet; but he was in despair at being condemned for treason, and at seeing the beautiful lady and his two friends imprisoned for a crime which he had not committed. He was not allowed to produce evidence, because his notebook was evidence enough. That was the law of Babylon. He was sent to execution through a crowd of spectators, of whom none dared to show pity for him, and who were gathered to see both how he bore himself and whether he made a good end. His family alone were grieved, because they could inherit nothing from a condemned criminal. Three-quarters of his estate was confiscated to the King, and the remaining quarter was assigned to Green Eyes.

Just as he was preparing for death, the King's parrot flew from the royal balcony and perched on a rosebush in Zadig's garden. A peach had been carried by the wind from a neighbouring tree, and had fallen on a piece of writing paper, to which it had stuck. The bird picked up the peach and the paper, and deposited them on the knees of its royal master. The Prince had the curiosity to read what was written on the paper. It made no sense, yet it seemed to be the ends of verses. He loved poetry, and there is always a resource for princes who love verse: the parrot's adventures set him musing. The Queen remembered what had been written on

Zadig's piece of paper, and had it brought. The two pieces were put together. They fitted exactly, and these were the verses as Zadig had written them:

> By most abandoned riot the land has been distressed;
> Confirmed upon the throne, the king has now no peer.
> In times of public quiet Love only makes unrest;
> He is the foe alone whom now we need to fear.

The King immediately ordered Zadig to be brought before him, and directed that the beautiful lady and the two friends should be released from prison. Zadig prostrated himself at the feet of the King and Queen, and most humbly begged pardon for having composed such bad verses. He spoke so gracefully, and with such wit and good sense, that the King and Queen determined to see more of him. He came again, and gave even greater satisfaction. For unjustly accusing him, Green Eyes was made to hand over to Zadig his whole estate; but Zadig gave it back to him, and Green Eyes' only pleasure was that he had not lost it. The King's regard for Zadig grew from day to day. He shared all his pleasures with him, and consulted him in all his affairs. The Queen treated him from that time with a degree of kindness which could have been dangerous to her, to the King her royal husband, to Zadig, and to the kingdom. And as for Zadig, he began to think that it was not so difficult to be happy after all.

CHAPTER 5

*

THE CONTEST IN GENEROSITY

THE time drew near for the celebration of a great festival
which took place every five years. It was the custom in Babylon at the end of the fifth year to make a solemn proclama-
tion declaring which citizen had performed the most generous
deed. The nobles and the mages were judges. The chief
satrap and governor of the city publicly announced the most
splendid deeds which had taken place under his rule. These
were put to the vote, and the King pronounced judgement.
People came to witness this ceremony from all corners of the
earth. The victor received from the monarch's hands a golden
cup set with jewels, and the King addressed him in these
words: 'Receive the reward of generosity, and may the Gods
give me many subjects like you!'

When this memorable day arrived, the King ascended his
throne, surrounded by the nobles, the mages, and the dele-
gates of all nations who had assembled to witness a contest
where glory was to be achieved not by swiftness of horses, or
by strength of body, but by virtue alone. The chief satrap
loudly proclaimed those deeds deserving the inestimable
prize. He did not mention Zadig's magnanimity in giving
back Green Eyes the whole of his fortune, for that was not
considered to be sufficiently noteworthy.

He first presented a judge who had passed sentence against
a plaintiff by an error for which he was in no way responsible.
To make amends, he had then given him all his property,
though it was of the same value as that which the plaintiff
had lost.

He next produced a young man who had married his
mistress to a friend. He was devoted to the lady, but his

37

friend was dying of love for her. And he had paid her dowry too.

Next he presented a soldier who had shown an even greater example of generosity in the Hyrcanian war. The enemy had attempted to seize his mistress, and he was defending her, when news reached him that not far away some other Hyrcanians had seized his mother. He left his mistress in tears, and rushed to his mother's assistance; but when he was able to return to his loved one, he found her dying. He was about to kill himself, but his mother declared that she had no one else to look after her, and he found the courage to go on living.

The judges were inclined towards the soldier, but the King intervened and said:

'His was certainly a noble action, and so were those of the others. But they do not give me any surprise; whereas yesterday a deed of Zadig's did surprise me. A few days ago I dismissed Coreb, my chief minister and favourite. I bitterly complained about his behaviour, and all my courtiers assured me that I had treated him too mildly: indeed they vied with each other in maligning him. I asked Zadig what he thought of Coreb, and he had the courage to speak well of him. I can recall examples in history of men who have paid for a mistake with their whole estate, who have given their mistresses away, who have preferred their mothers to the objects of their affection; but I have never read of a courtier supporting a disgraced minister who had put his Sovereign in a rage. I award twenty thousand pieces of gold to those whose generous deeds have just been recited, but I award the cup to Zadig.'

'Sire,' said he to the King, 'it is your Majesty alone who deserves the cup, for your deed is quite unprecedented! You are a King, and yet you were in no way angry with your slave, when he opposed you in your wrath.'

The King's praises were in everyone's mouth, and so were Zadig's. The judge who had given up his estate, the lover who had married his mistress to his friend, the soldier who had preferred his mother's safety to his mistress's, all received their awards at the King's hand and saw their names inscribed in the Roll of Generosity. Zadig had the cup, and the King gained the reputation of being a good Prince, though he did not long retain it. The day was solemnized by festivities which lasted longer than the law provided for, and the memory of it is still preserved in Asia. Zadig remarked: 'Now at last I am happy'; but he was mistaken.

CHAPTER 6

*

THE MINISTER

THE King had lost his Chief Minister, and chose Zadig to fill his place. The beautiful ladies of Babylon unanimously applauded his choice, for since the foundation of the Empire there had never been a Minister so young. The courtiers were angry to a man; Green Eyes broke a blood vessel, and his nose swelled to extraordinary proportions. When Zadig had expressed his thanks to the King and Queen, he went to thank the parrot too.

'Beautiful bird,' said he, 'it is you who have saved my life, you who have made me Chief Minister. The Queen's bitch and the King's horse had done me grievous injury; but you have been my benefactor. On such threads as these hang the destinies of men! But,' he added, 'such strange good fortune, perhaps, will soon vanish away.'

'Aye,' said the parrot.

Zadig was surprised at this reply; but as a natural philosopher he did not believe that parrots were prophets. His mind was soon at rest, and he began to discharge his new duties to the best of his ability.

He made everyone feel the sacred authority of the law without making the weight of his own dignity felt. He never thwarted the decisions of the Privy Council, and each Vizier was free to express his opinion without displeasing him. When he tried a case, it was not he who gave judgement but the law. Yet when the law was too severe, he relaxed it; and when no law existed, his decision might have been taken for that of Zoroaster.

It is from Zadig that nations have derived the great principle that it is better to risk acquitting a criminal than to condemn an innocent man. He believed that laws were made as much to protect the King's subjects as to deter them from crime. His principal talent was in diffusing those truths which everyone tries to conceal, and from his first days in office he put this great talent into use. A famous Babylonian merchant had died in India. He had divided his estate between his two sons, after arranging for their sister's marriage, and had left a sum of thirty thousand pieces of gold to whichever of his two sons was deemed to love him best. The elder built a tomb for his father; the younger used part of his legacy to increase his sister's dowry. Everyone said: 'It is the elder son who loves his father best: the younger son prefers his sister. So the thirty thousand pieces of gold should belong to the elder.'

Zadig summoned them both to see him, one after the other. He said to the elder son:

'Your father is not dead after all. He has recovered from his illness, and is returning to Babylon.'

'Thank God!' exclaimed the young man. 'But I have spent a lot of money on that tomb.'

Zadig then said the same thing to the younger son.

'Thank God!' he replied. 'I am going to return all the money to my father. But I hope he will let my sister keep what I have given her.'

'You shall give nothing back,' said Zadig. 'The thirty thousand pieces are yours. It is you who love your father best.'

A rich young woman who had made a promise of marriage to two mages had been receiving instruction for a few months from each of them, and found herself with child. Both mages wished to marry her.

'I shall take as my husband,' she said, 'the one who has put me in the position of presenting the Empire with a subject.'

'Mine is the good work,' said one of the mages.

'The honour is mine,' said the other.

41

'Very well,' she replied. 'I shall recognize as the child's father whichever of you can give him the better education.'

She gave birth to a son; and since each of the mages wanted to educate him, the case was brought before Zadig. He summoned the two mages, and said to the first:

'What will you teach your pupil?'

'I will teach him,' said the Doctor, 'the eight parts of Rhetoric, Dialectics, Astrology, and Demonology. I shall explain to him what is meant by Substance and Accidence, Abstract and Concrete, Monads and Pre-established Harmony.'

'I,' said the second mage, 'shall try to give him a sense of justice and make him worthy of having friends.'

At which Zadig declared:

'Whether or not you are his father, you shall marry his mother.'

CHAPTER 7

*

DISPUTES AND AUDIENCES

THUS every day he gave proof of his subtle wit and bountiful nature. He was generally admired; he was even loved. In fact he was regarded as the most fortunate of men. The whole empire resounded with his name. Not a woman but made eyes at him, not a man but commended his decisions; the learned regarded him as their oracle, and the priests even declared that he knew more than old Yebor the Archimage. There was no more risk of being had up for dangerous talk about griffins, since people believed only what to him seemed credible.

There had been a great dispute in Babylon which had lasted for 1,500 years and had divided the empire into two rival sects. One held that you must never enter the temple of Mithras except on the left foot; the other held this practice in abomination and never entered except on the right. Everyone waited for the solemn festival of the sacred fire, to see which sect Zadig belonged to. The world had its eyes fixed on his two feet, and the whole town waited in great suspense. Zadig leapt into the temple, both feet together, and he proceeded to prove in an eloquent sermon that the God of Heaven and Earth has no favourites and cares no more for the left leg than the right. Green Eyes and his wife maintained that his sermon was weak in figures of speech, that he had not made the mountains and the little hills dance enough. 'His manner is dry and unimaginative,' they said. 'With him you cannot see the ocean put to flight, the stars fall, or the sun melt like wax. He does not command a good Oriental style.' Zadig was content with a style based on good sense. Everyone was on his side; not because he was getting on well, nor because he was a sensible and likable man, but because he was Grand Vizier.

He was equally successful in bringing to an end the great dispute between the White and the Black Mages. The White Mages maintained that it was irreverent at times of prayer to turn towards the east in winter. The Black Mages were confident that God detested the prayers of those who turned towards the setting sun in summer. Zadig decided that a man could turn which way he pleased.

He discovered the secret of transacting his public and private business in the morning, and thus he was able to devote the rest of the day to the cultural improvement of Babylon. He had tragedies produced which excited tears, and comedies which provoked laughter. They had long been out of date; but he revived them because he had good taste. He did not pretend to know better than the actors, but rewarded them with favours and distinctions, and cherished no secret jealousy of their talents. In the evenings he entertained the King and Queen – the Queen particularly. The King used to exclaim, 'What a fine statesman he is!'; the Queen would murmur, 'Isn't he charming!'; and both would add, 'It would have been a great pity if he had been hanged!'

Never had a statesman been obliged to give so many audiences to the ladies. Most of them came to talk to him about non-existent affairs, so as to have one with him. Madam Green Eyes was one of the first to seek an audience. She swore by Mithras, Vesta, and the sacred flame that she loathed her husband's conduct, and she then revealed how jealous and brutal he was. She even gave him to understand that the Gods had punished Green Eyes by refusing him the precious consequences of that vestal flame by which alone man can make himself one of the immortals. As she finished speaking, she dropped her garter. Zadig picked it up with his customary politeness, but he did not replace it above the lady's knee; and this little mistake, if it can be called a mistake, was the cause of terrible misfortunes. Zadig never gave it a thought, but Madam Green Eyes pondered it deeply.

Other ladies sought audience every day. The secret annals of Babylon claim that he once succumbed, but that he was surprised to find that he enjoyed his mistress without pleasure, and embraced her absentmindedly. The lady on whom he almost unwittingly bestowed his favour was one of Queen Astarte's maids of honour. The poor little thing consoled herself by reflecting that the great man must be deeply engrossed with affairs of state to brood upon them even when making love. At a moment when most people say nothing and others only murmur a few sacred words, Zadig blurted out, 'The Queen.' His partner fancied that the pleasures of the moment had at last brought him to his senses, and that what he had said to her was: 'My Queen.' But Zadig, still absentminded, uttered the name Astarte. The lady construed everything to her own advantage at this blissful juncture, and supposed that what he meant was: 'You are more beautiful than Queen Astarte.' She left Zadig's seraglio loaded with beautiful gifts, and went to recount her adventures to Madam Green Eyes, who was her close friend. That lady was deeply offended at Zadig's preference: 'He did not even replace this garter for me. I won't use it any more.'

'Oh, look!' said the more fortunate lady. 'You have the same garters as the Queen! You must go to the same maker, then?'

This set Madam Green Eyes thinking. She made no reply, and went off to talk with her husband.

In the meanwhile Zadig found that his attention used to wander when he gave audiences, and in the seat of justice. He did not know how to account for it; that was his only trouble. He had a dream in which he seemed to be lying on a bed of dry grass, some of which pricked him and made him uncomfortable; then he was lying softly on a bed of roses, from which a serpent issued and stung him to the heart with its sharp and venomous fang.

'Yes,' said he to himself, 'for long enough my bed was dry and prickly, and now it is as soft as roses. But what will the serpent turn out to be?'

JEALOUSY

ZADIG's misfortunes arose partly from his good fortune, but even more from his attainments. Every day he had an audience with the King and with Astarte his peerless consort. The charm of his conversation was increased by an ambition to please, which is to wit what ornament is to beauty. His youth and natural charm gradually made an impression upon Astarte, which at first she did not recognize. Passion flourished in her innocent breast; she gave herself up without reflexion and without fear to the pleasure of seeing and listening to a man favoured by her husband as well as by the state. She was never tired of commending him to the King; and she talked about him to her ladies, who were even more extravagant in their praises. All this served to bury within her heart the arrow she did not feel. The presents she gave to Zadig smacked of flirtation more than she was aware. She fancied that she spoke to him only as a Queen grateful for his services, but sometimes her expression was that of a woman in love.

Astarte was much more beautiful than that Semira who had so strongly disliked one-eyed men, or the other woman who had wanted to cut off her husband's nose. The intimacy which Astarte permitted, the tender words which raised a blush in her cheeks, the glances which she vainly tried to avert from his — all this kindled in Zadig's heart a flame which surprised him. He fought against it. He summoned to his aid the philosophy which had always helped him. But philosophy could only shed light; it could not provide relief. Duty, Gratitude, Offended Majesty, all appeared in his eyes like Avenging Furies. He continued to struggle, and he triumphed; but the victory which he had to maintain unceasingly cost him some groans and tears. He no longer dared to address the Queen with that gentle freedom which held such charms for both of them. His eyes no longer sparkled; his speech was constrained and disjointed, and his gaze was fixed upon the ground. But sometimes he could not help stealing a glance at Astarte, and found that her eyes, though wet with tears, still sparkled with affection. They seemed to say: 'We adore each other, and are afraid of our love; we are the slaves of a passion of which we disapprove.'

Zadig left the Queen's presence with a mind bewildered and distracted, and a heart weighed down by a burden he could no longer bear. Swept by the force of these emotions, he betrayed his secret to his friend Cador, as a man might do who has long suffered attacks of pain and at last reveals his suffering by crying out at some excruciating spasm, and by the cold sweat pouring from his forehead.

Cador said to him: 'I have already discerned those feelings which you would like to hide even from yourself, for the passions show signs which cannot be misinterpreted. Consider, my dear Zadig; if I can read your heart, will not the King read it also and discover feelings which are sure to offend him? He has only one fault; but that is that he's the most jealous man alive. You control your passion with more strength than the Queen can muster against hers, because you are a philosopher, and because you are Zadig. Astarte is a woman; she lets her eyes speak all the more imprudently, in that she is as yet unaware of guilt. She is convinced of her own innocence, and unfortunately she does not preserve appearances. I shall tremble for her as long as she has nothing to reproach herself with. If you were both agreed, you could deceive us all. A newborn passion will manifest itself, especially if it is resisted; but love which is satisfied knows how to conceal itself.'

Zadig shuddered at the notion of betraying the King his benefactor; and never was he more faithful to his prince than when guilty of an involuntary crime. But the Queen so often uttered the name of Zadig, and blushed so profusely as she did so; she was alternately so animated and so confused when speaking to him in the King's presence; she became so deeply engrossed in thought when he retired, that the King was disturbed. He believed all he saw; and what he did not see he imagined. He noticed in particular that his wife's slippers were blue, and that Zadig's slippers were blue; he also noticed that his wife's ribbons were yellow, and that Zadig's cap was yellow also. Terrible indications, these, for a touchy prince. Suspicion changed to certainty in his embittered mind.

As every slave in a royal household is also engaged in spying upon the hearts of his master and mistress, it was soon recognized that Astarte was in love, and that Moabdar was jealous. Green Eyes persuaded Madam Green Eyes to send the King that garter of hers which looked like the Queen's. To make matters worse the garter was blue. The Monarch's only thought was of revenge. One night he decided to poison the Queen, and to have Zadig strangled, at day-break. The order was given to a pitiless eunuch, always employed to execute the King's vengeance.

In the King's chamber there was a little dwarf, who was dumb but not deaf. Everyone tolerated him, and he was a witness of the most secret proceedings, as though he were a domestic animal. This little dumb creature was very fond of the Queen and of Zadig. His horror was as great as his surprise when he heard the order given for their death. But what could he do to prevent this terrible order, which was to be put into effect within a few hours? He did not know how to write; but he had learned to paint, and he was especially good at catching a likeness. He spent part of the night drawing what he wanted the Queen to understand. His sketch showed the King transfigured with rage in one corner of the picture, giving orders to his eunuch; a blue rope and a jug stood on a table, with blue garters and yellow ribbons; in the middle of the picture the Queen was dying in the arms of her women, and Zadig lay strangled at her feet. The horizon showed the sun rising, to indicate that this horrible execution was due to take place at dawn. As soon as he had finished he ran to the apartment of Astarte's waiting-woman, woke her up, and made her understand that this picture was to be taken to the Queen that very instant.

In the middle of the night there was a knock at Zadig's door. He was awakened and given a note from the Queen. Zadig opened the letter with trembling hands, wondering whether he was dreaming. It is impossible to express his surprise, his consternation, the utter despair which overcame him, on reading these words:

Fly this instant, or you will lose your life. Fly, Zadig, I command you, in the name of our love and of my yellow ribbons. I am quite innocent, but I fear that I shall die the death of a criminal.

Zadig had scarcely strength enough to speak. He sent for Cador, and without saying a word handed him the Queen's note. Cador urged him to obey its instructions and to set out immediately for Memphis.

'If you dare to go and find the Queen,' said he, 'you will hasten her death. If you speak to the King, you will certainly lose her. I will take charge of her destiny: follow your own. I will spread the rumour that you have set out for India. I shall soon come and find you, and tell you what has happened in Babylon.'

At the same time, Cador ordered two of the swiftest dromedaries to be brought to a secret door of the palace. He placed Zadig in the saddle; indeed he had had to carry him, for he was almost ready to expire. One servant accompanied him, and he was soon lost to his friend's sight. Cador then retraced his steps, overcome with astonishment and grief.

When he reached the brow of a hill from which Babylon could be seen, the illustrious fugitive turned his eyes towards the Queen's palace, and fainted. He came to his senses only to shed tears and to wish for death. At last, after brooding upon the pitiful fate of the most amiable of women and the most eminent of Queens, he began to reflect upon his own condition, and exclaimed:

'What then is human life? And of what use has virtue been to me? Two women have basely deceived me. The third, who is innocent, and more beautiful than either, is about to die. All the good I have done has brought curses upon me, and I have been raised to the summit of grandeur only to fall into the most horrible pit of misfortune. If I had been wicked, as so many others are, I should have been happy like them.'

Overwhelmed by these melancholy reflexions, his eyes clouded with grief, the pallor of death upon his face, his spirit dejected by sombre despair, he resumed his journey towards Egypt.

CHAPTER 9

*

THE BEATEN WOMAN

ZADIG took his course by the stars. The constellation of Orion and the brilliance of Sirius directed his steps towards Canopus. He was lost in admiration for these vast spheres of light, which look to our eyes like feeble sparks only because the Earth, which is in reality a mere imperceptible point in the Universe, appears to our greedy outlook something noble and grand. Then he pictured to himself men as they really are, insects devouring one another on a tiny fragment of mud. The truth of this conception seemed to annihilate his misfortunes as he recalled to mind the utter nothingness of his own being and of Babylon too. His spirit soared into space; and with the grossness of the senses left behind, he meditated upon the unchangeable laws of the heavenly universe. But when he returned to himself a moment later, and looked into his heart, and thought that Astarte had perhaps perished for his sake, the Universe disappeared from his view, and all he saw in the whole range of Nature was Astarte dying and his ill-fated self.

While surrendering himself alternately to sublime philosophy and overwhelming grief, he drew near to the frontiers of Egypt; his faithful servant had already reached the first settlement, and was looking for lodgings there. Meanwhile Zadig took a walk towards the gardens at the edge of the village. Not far from the road he saw a woman in tears, crying aloud to Heaven and Earth for help, and pursued by a man in a violent temper. She had just been overtaken by the man, and had thrown herself at his feet, with her arms round his knees; but the fellow loaded her with blows and reproaches. Judging by the Egyptian's violence and by the

lady's repeated appeals for pardon, Zadig took the one to be
jealous and the other unfaithful; but when he regarded the
lady, who was strikingly beautiful and even bore some resemblance to the unfortunate Astarte, he felt moved by compassion for her, and was horrified at the Egyptian.

'Help me,' she cried to Zadig amidst her sobs. 'Deliver me
from the hands of the most barbarous of men, and save my
life!'

At this appeal he ran and threw himself between her and
the cruel wretch. He had some knowledge of the Egyptian
tongue; and addressing him in that language, he said:

'If you have any humanity, I conjure you to be merciful
to weakness and beauty. How could you treat this masterpiece of nature so cruelly! She is at your feet, and she has no
defence but her tears!'

'Oho!' said the fellow, in a transport of rage. 'So you are
sweet upon her too! I'll have my revenge on you, then.'

With those words, he let go the lady, whom he was holding
by the hair, and tried to stab the stranger with his lance.
Zadig, whose temper was cool, had no difficulty in avoiding
an angry man's attack, and seized the lance by its iron tip.
While the one tried to snatch it away and the other tried
to get possession of it, the lance broke in their hands. At that,
the Egyptian drew his sword; Zadig did likewise, and they
fell upon each other. The former dealt a hundred violent
blows, which the latter skilfully parried. Meanwhile the lady
sat down on the grass, tidied her hair, and watched them.
The Egyptian was more robust than his adversary, but Zadig
was more adroit. He fought skilfully, his brain guiding his
arm, while the other fought like a maniac whose blind rage
directs his movements at random. Zadig made a pass at him,
and disarmed him. This made the Egyptian more furious;
but while trying to fling himself upon his opponent, he was
seized by Zadig, who pressed home the attack and brought
him to the ground. Then, with a sword at the Egyptian's
breast, Zadig offered him his life. The Egyptian was beside

himself with rage; drawing his dagger, he wounded Zadig with it at the moment when his victor was offering him mercy. Roused to indignation, Zadig plunged his sword into the man's breast, and the Egyptian, uttering a horrible cry, fell back and died. Zadig then approached the lady, and gently said to her:

'He forced me to kill him. I have avenged you, and you are delivered from the most violent man I ever saw. What would you have of me now, madam?'

'Your death, you villain!' she replied, 'your death! You have slain my lover. I could tear your heart out!'

'Indeed, madam,' replied Zadig, 'that's a strange man to have for a lover. He was beating you as hard as he could, and he wanted to take my life because you begged me to come to your help.'

'I wish he were still alive to beat me,' cried the lady. 'I deserved it, for I had given him cause to be jealous. Would to God he were beating me, and you were in his place!'

Zadig was more surprised and angry than he had ever been in his life. 'Madam,' said he, 'beautiful as you are, it would serve you right if I were to beat you now myself, since you talk so absurdly. But I shall not give myself the trouble.'

Thereupon he remounted his camel and set off for the town. He had not gone far before he turned round on hearing the noise of four horsemen, couriers from Babylon, who were riding at full speed. One of them noticed the woman, and cried, 'That's her. She is just like the description we've been given.' They took no heed of the dead man, and unceremoniously laid hold of the lady, whereupon she kept calling to Zadig: 'Help me once more, generous stranger! Forgive me for reproaching you. Help me, and I am yours till death.'

But Zadig's desire to fight for her was now gratified. 'It's other people's turn,' he replied. 'You won't catch me again.' Besides, he was wounded and bleeding, and had need of attention; and the sight of four Babylonians, probably sent by King Moabdar, filled him with disquiet. He hastened towards the village, unable to conceive why four couriers from Babylon should come and arrest this Egyptian woman, and rapt in astonishment at the character of the lady herself.

CHAPTER 10

*

SLAVERY

WHEN he entered the Egyptian village, he found himself surrounded by people crying: 'There's the man who ran off with the lovely Missouf and murdered Cletophis!'

'Gentlemen,' said he, 'God forbid that I should ever run off with your lovely Missouf; she's too fickle for me. And as for Cletophis, I assure you I didn't murder him; I merely defended myself. He tried to kill me, because I humbly asked him to have mercy on the lovely Missouf, whom he was beating so pitilessly. I am a stranger, and have come to take sanctuary in Egypt. It's not likely that, in coming to ask your protection, I should begin by running off with a woman and murdering a man.'

At that time the Egyptians had a sense of justice and humanity. They led Zadig to the town hall, where first his wound was dressed; he and his servant were then separately questioned to discover the truth. Zadig was found to be no murderer; but he was guilty of shedding blood, and was sentenced by law to be a slave. His two camels were sold for the benefit of the community; all the gold he had about him was distributed amongst the villagers; and both he and his travelling companion were put up for sale in the market square. An Arabian merchant called Setoc was the highest bidder, but the manservant fetched a better price than his master, because he was better fitted for hard work. Indeed there was no comparison between the two men, and Zadig was therefore ranked below his servant. They were chained together by the ankles, and in this wise they followed the Arabian merchant to his house. On the way Zadig consoled his servant, and bid him have patience; but as his habit was, he made some reflexions on the life of man.

'I see,' said he to his servant, 'that the unhappiness of my fate has encroached upon yours. So far, everything has taken a peculiar turn for me. I have been fined for not noticing a bitch; I thought I was to be burnt at the stake for a griffin; I have been condemned to execution for making verses in praise of the King; I was very nearly strangled because the Queen had yellow ribbons; and here we are in slavery, you and I, just because a brutal fellow beat his mistress. Well, we mustn't be discouraged! Perhaps there'll be an end to it all! Arabian merchants must necessarily have slaves, and why should not I be one as much as another, since I am as much a man as another? This merchant will not be harsh to us; he must treat his slaves well, if he wants to use them.'

These were his words, but at the bottom of his heart he was wondering what had happened to the Queen of Babylon.

Two days later, Setoc the Merchant left for the Arabian desert with his slaves and his camels. His tribe lived near the desert of Horeb, and the route was long and wearisome. On the journey, Setoc rated the manservant higher than his master because he knew more about loading camels, and accordingly he received every little favour.

A camel died two days' journey from Horeb, and its load was distributed over each slave's back; Zadig took his share. When he saw his slaves bent under their burdens, Setoc started laughing; but Zadig took the liberty of explaining the reason, and told him about the laws of equilibrium. The merchant was astonished, and began to take a different view of him. Seeing that he had excited his curiosity, Zadig increased it by teaching him many things he knew about the merchant's line of business, such as the specific gravity of equal volumes of metals and other materials, the characteristics of several useful animals, and the method of training those that are not useful. In short, Zadig gained the reputation of a sage, and Setoc gave him preference over the fellow-slave he had so highly rated. He treated him well, and had no cause to repent of it.

Once more amongst his own people, Setoc demanded repayment of five hundred ounces of silver which he had lent to a Jew in the presence of two witnesses; but since both witnesses were dead, and the debt could not be proved, the Jew appropriated the merchant's money and thanked God for enabling him to cheat an Arab. Setoc mentioned his difficulty to Zadig, who had now become his adviser.

'Whereabouts was it,' asked Zadig, 'that you lent your five hundred ounces of silver to this infidel?'

'On a large stone,' replied the merchant, 'near Mount Horeb.'

'What sort of a character has your debtor?' said Zadig.

'He's a swindler,' replied Setoc.

'Yes,' said Zadig. 'But what I am asking you is whether he is quick-witted or dull. Is he cautious, or is he imprudent?'

'Of all the welshers I've ever known, he's the smartest,' said the merchant.

'Very well,' replied Zadig, 'allow me to plead your cause before the Judge.'

Thereupon he summoned the Jew before the Tribunal, and addressed the Judge as follows:

'Most gracious Cushion upon the Throne of Equity, I have come to sue this man, in the name of my master, for five hundred ounces of silver which he will not repay.'

'Have you any witnesses?' asked the Judge.

'No, they are dead; but there remains a large stone on which the silver was counted. If it please your Honour to give orders that the stone be fetched, I hope it will bear witness. The Jew and I will stay here until the stone arrives. I shall send for it at the expense of Setoc my master.'

'Very well,' said the Judge, who then proceeded to other business.

At the end of the session, the Judge addressed Zadig, and said:

'So your stone has not arrived yet?'

The Jew laughed at this, and replied:

'If Your Honour were to stay here till tomorrow, the stone would still not have arrived; it's more than six miles from here, and it would need fifteen men to remove it.'

'Well,' cried Zadig, 'I was quite right in saying that the stone would bear witness; since this man knows where it is, he admits that the silver was counted upon it.'

This so much disconcerted the Jew that he was soon forced to make a clean breast of it. The Judge ordered that he should be bound to the stone, without food or drink, until he gave back the five hundred ounces. They were soon paid.

The slave Zadig and the stone were held in great esteem throughout Arabia.

CHAPTER II

*

THE FUNERAL PYRE

SETOC was delighted, and made an intimate friend of his slave. Like the King of Babylon, he could no longer do without him; and Zadig was glad that Setoc had no wife. He discovered that his master was naturally benevolent, and possessed a large measure of honesty and good sense; but he was displeased to see him worshipping the celestial host, that is to say the Sun, the Moon, and the Stars, as the ancient custom is in Arabia. He spoke to him about it with great discretion on several occasions. At length he told him that these bodies were in no way supernatural, and deserved no more homage than a rock or a tree.

'But,' said Setoc, 'they are eternal beings from which we derive all benefits: they give life to Nature, they rule the seasons, and they are besides so far-removed from us that one can't help revering them.'

'You derive more good,' replied Zadig, 'from the waters of the Red Sea which bears your merchandise to the Indies. Why shouldn't that be as old as the stars? And if you worship what is so remote, you ought to worship the land of the Gangarides, which is at the other end of the world.'

'No,' said Setoc. 'The stars are so brilliant that I cannot help worshipping them.'

That same evening Zadig lit a great number of candles in the tent where he was to have supper with Setoc, and as soon as his patron arrived, he fell upon his knees before the lighted tapers, and addressed them thus:

'Bright and everlasting luminaries, look ever favourably upon me.'

Having uttered these words, he sat down to table without taking any notice of Setoc.

'What on earth are you doing?' said Setoc to him in astonishment.

'I am doing what you do,' replied Zadig. 'I am worshipping these candles, and I am taking no notice of their master and mine.'

Setoc perceived the meaning underlying this performance. His slave's wisdom entered into his soul, and instead of wasting incense on the objects of Creation, he worshipped the Eternal Being who made them.

There was at that time in Arabia a horrible custom which originally came from Scythia; it had been established in India by the authority of the Brahmins, and threatened to overrun the whole of the East. When a married man died and his devoted wife wished to be assured of sanctification, she burnt herself alive in public on the body of her husband. It was a solemn festival, and was called the Pyre of Widowhood. The tribe which could claim the greatest number of burned women was the most respected. An Arab of Setoc's tribe had died; and his widow, Almona, a very devout woman, had announced the day and hour when she would throw herself into the fire to the sound of tambours and trumpets. Zadig represented to Setoc that this horrible custom was contrary to the welfare of the human race; he pointed out that every day young widows were allowed to be burned who could have produced children for the State, or who could at least have brought up their own; and he made him agree that if possible such a barbarous custom should be abolished. But Setoc replied:

'For more than a thousand years women have had the right to burn themselves. Which of us shall dare to alter a law which time has consecrated? Is there anything more respectable than an ancient abuse?'

'Reason is more ancient,' replied Zadig. 'Speak to the leaders of the tribes, while I go and find the young widow.'

He gained admission to her, and after ingratiating himself with praise of her beauty, and saying what a pity it was that so many charms should be committed to the flames, he praised her still more for her constancy and courage.

'You must have been devoted to your husband,' he said to her.

'Indeed I wasn't,' replied the Arabian lady. 'He was a brutal creature, consumed with jealousy, a quite insufferable fellow; but I am firmly resolved to throw myself upon his funeral pyre.'

'There must evidently be a most delicious pleasure in being burnt alive,' said Zadig.

'Ah,' said the lady, 'it makes me tremble to think of it, but it has to be endured. I am a devout woman, and I should lose my reputation. Everyone would laugh at me if I did not burn myself.'

After making her agree that she was going to burn herself in deference to others and to gratify her vanity, Zadig spoke to her at length in such a way as to make her feel some love of living. He even succeeded in arousing in her a measure of goodwill towards himself.

'Well, then, what will you do,' he said, 'if you decide not to make this useless sacrifice?'

The lady sighed, as she answered: 'I think I should beg you to marry me.'

This declaration made no appeal to Zadig, whose mind was still possessed by the image of Astarte; but he went immediately to find the leaders of the tribes and tell them what had happened. He advised them to make a law forbidding a widow to burn herself until after she had conversed in private with a young man for the space of a whole hour. Since that time not a woman in Arabia has burnt herself alive. To Zadig alone was the credit due of having destroyed in one day such a cruel custom, which had lasted for so many centuries. He was therefore the benefactor of Arabia.

CHAPTER 12

*

THE SUPPER PARTY

SETOC, who could not bear to be parted from the man with whom wisdom had taken up her abode, brought him to the Great Fair of Balsora, where all the greatest merchants of the habitable world were accustomed to meet. For Zadig it was a source of delight to see so many men from different countries met together in one place. It seemed to him that the universe was one large family, which had assembled at Balsora. He was seated at table on the second day with an Egyptian, an Indian from the banks of the Ganges, an inhabitant of Cathay, a Greek, a Celt, and several other strangers who in their frequent journeys to the Arabian Gulf had learnt enough Arabic to make themselves understood. The Egyptian seemed to be in a great rage.

'What an odious country Balsora is!' he exclaimed. 'I have been refused a thousand ounces of gold on the best security in the world.'

'Indeed!' said Setoc. 'What security did you offer, that you were refused such a sum?'

'Nothing less than my aunt's body,' replied the Egyptian. 'And she was the handsomest woman in Egypt. She used to accompany me everywhere; but she died on the way, and I had her made into the most beautiful mummy. In my own country I should get all I wanted with her as deposit. It's very strange that here they won't even give me a thousand ounces of gold on such solid security.'

Angry as he was, he was going to help himself to an excellent boiled fowl, when the Indian took him by the hand and sorrowfully exclaimed:

'What are you going to do?'

'I am going to eat a bit of this fowl,' said the man with the mummy.

'Do be careful,' replied the man from the Ganges. 'It may very well happen that the dead woman's soul has entered the body of this fowl, and you would not wish to be in danger of eating your aunt. To have fowls cooked is the clearest outrage upon Nature.'

'What do you mean, with your Nature and your fowls?' replied the testy Egyptian. 'We worship a bull, and we eat it too.'

'You worship a bull! Oh, surely not!' said the man from the Ganges.

'Certainly we do,' replied the other. 'What's more, we have been doing it for a hundred and thirty-five thousand years, and none of us see anything wrong in it.'

'A hundred and thirty-five thousand years!' said the Indian. 'That's a bit of an exaggeration. It is only eighty thousand years since India was first inhabited, and we are certainly a more ancient race than you are. Besides, Brahma forbade us to eat oxen before you had ever thought of putting them on your altars and your spits.'

'Your Brahma's a ridiculous creature to be compared with Apis!' said the Egyptian. 'What has Brahma done to boast of?'

'It was he,' the Brahmin replied, 'who taught men to read and write, and to whom the whole world is indebted for the game of chess.'

'You are mistaken,' said a Chaldean sitting near him. 'It is to the fish Oannes that we owe these great benefits, and it is not right to offer homage to any but him. Everyone will tell you that he was a divine being with a golden tail and a beautiful human head, who rose from the water to come and preach on earth for three hours every day. He had several children, all of whom were Kings, as everyone knows. I have his portrait at home, which I worship as in duty bound. You can eat as much beef as you like, but it is certainly a gross impiety to cook fish; though really you are both of too recent and ignoble origin for me to dispute with. The Egyptian nation goes back only one hundred and thirty-five thousand years, and the Indians cannot boast of more than eighty thousand, whereas we have almanacks eighty centuries old. So take my advice: give up your follies, and I will present each of you with a beautiful portrait of Oannes.'

The man from Cambalu then began to speak, and said:

'I have a great respect for the Egyptians, the Chaldeans, the Greeks, the Celts, Brahma, the bull Apis, and the beautiful fish Oannes; but Li, or Tien,* as we should prefer to call him, surely ranks higher than bulls and fish. I shall say nothing about my country; it is as big as Egypt, Chaldea, and the Indies put together. I shall not dispute its age, because it is enough to be happy, and it is of small moment to be old; but if there were need to talk of almanacks, I should say that the whole of Asia accepts ours, and that we had very good ones before arithmetic was known in Chaldea.'

'What a lot of ignorant fellows you are,' exclaimed the Greek. 'Don't you know that Chaos is the father of all, and that form and matter have brought the world to the state it is now in?'

The Greek spoke for a long time, but at last he was interrupted by the Celt, who had drunk a good deal while the dispute was going on, and so believed that he was wiser than the others. He swore an oath and said it was only Teutath and the mistletoe on the oak tree that were worth discussing, and that for his part he always carried a piece of mistletoe in his pocket. He added that his ancestors the Scythians were the only honest people there had ever been on the earth, that admittedly they had often eaten men, but that that did not prevent their nation from being held in great respect; and lastly that if anyone spoke ill of Teutath, he would teach him better manners. Upon this the quarrel grew warm, and

* Chinese words, whose proper meaning is: *Li*, the light of nature, or reason; and *Tien*, the sky. They also mean God. [Voltaire's note.]

Setoc feared bloodshed at the table. Zadig, who had kept silent throughout the dispute, rose to his feet at last. He addressed the Celt first, since he was the most angry. He told him that he was right, and asked him for some mistletoe. He praised the Greek for his eloquence, and cooled the heat of the party. He said very little to the man from Cathay, because he had been the most reasonable of all. He then spoke to them as follows:

'My friends, you were going to quarrel about nothing; for you are all of the same opinion.'

At this they all protested.

'Isn't it true,' he said to the Celt, 'that what you worship is not this mistletoe, but him who made the mistletoe and the oak?'

'Yes, of course,' replied the Celt.

Then turning to the Egyptian, he said: 'What you revere is not really the bull himself but the giver of all good bulls. Is that so?'

'Yes,' said the Egyptian.

'The fish Oannes,' Zadig continued, 'ought to yield place to him who made the sea and the fish.'

'I quite agree,' said the Chaldean.

'The Indian and the Cathayan,' Zadig added, 'agree with you in recognizing a First Principle. I did not fully understand all the admirable things the Greek was saying, but I am sure that he too accepts a Supreme Being, upon whom form and matter depend.'

The Greek, who was generally admired, said that Zadig had fully comprehended his thought.

'Well then,' replied Zadig, 'you are all of the same opinion; and there is nothing to quarrel about in that.'

Everyone embraced him; and Setoc, after selling his merchandise at a good price, took Zadig back to his tribe. Zadig learnt on arrival that he had been tried in his absence and was to be burnt at the stake in a slow fire.

CHAPTER 13

*

THE ASSIGNATIONS

WHILE he was away at Balsora the Priests of the Stars had decided to punish him. The precious stones and jewellery of the young widows they sent to the pyre belonged to them by right; and it was the least they could do to have Zadig burnt for the bad turn he had served them. They therefore accused him of incorrect thinking about the Celestial Host; they entered depositions against him, and swore that they had heard him declare that the stars do not set in the sea. This frightful blasphemy made the judges tremble; they were ready to rend their clothes, and they would undoubtedly have done so if Zadig had been able to pay for them. But in their extreme displeasure they contented themselves with sentencing him to be burnt at a slow fire. Setoc, in despair, used all his authority to try to save his friend, but in vain; he was soon obliged to keep his peace. Almona, the young widow who had acquired a strong taste for life (which she owed to Zadig), resolved to rescue him from the funeral pyre, an evil custom whose futility he had proved to her. She pondered her scheme without speaking to anyone about it. Zadig was to be executed the following day; she had only that night to arrange his escape. This is how a prudent and charitable woman set to work.

She sprinkled herself with perfumes, and set off her natural charms with a rich and elegant robe. Thus attired, she went to crave a secret audience with the High Priest of the Stars. When she was admitted to the presence of this venerable old man, she addressed him in these words:

'Eldest Son of the Great Bear, Brother of the Bull, and Cousin of the Great Dog,' (these were the titles of this hierarch), 'I am come to confide to you some misgivings. I am much afraid that I have committed a terrible sin in not burning myself upon my dear husband's pyre. What, after all, had I to preserve? Some perishable flesh, already quite faded.'

As she spoke, she drew back her long silken sleeves and revealed two bare arms of lovely shape and dazzling whiteness.

'You see,' she said, 'how little it is worth.'

The High Priest found in his heart that it was worth a good deal. His eyes said so, and his mouth declared it; he swore that never in his life had he seen such beautiful arms.

'Ah, well!' sighed the widow. 'My arms may be a little less wretched than the rest; but you will admit that my neck was not worthy of the attentions I gave it.'

So saying she revealed the most beautiful bosom that Nature had ever made. It looked like an ivory apple decked with a rose-bud, though that would have appeared as dull as madder-flowers on boxwood by comparison; even the whiteness of freshly washed lambs jumping out of a clear pool would have seemed a dull yellow. That bosom, those large black eyes, softly shining with tender fire, cheeks glowing like beautiful carnations and fresh cream, a nose quite unlike the tower upon Mount Lebanon, lips like twin rows of coral framing the most lovely pearls of the Arabian sea – the general effect of it all was to make the old man think he was twenty years old. He tried to stammer out a tender declaration. Seeing his excitement, Almona craved pardon for Zadig. The old man heaved a sigh:

'Dearest lady,' said he, 'even if I were to grant you this favour, the pardon would be of no use. It must be signed by three of my colleagues.'

'Nevertheless,' said Almona, 'I beg you to sign.'

'Willingly,' said the Priest, 'on condition that your favours shall be the reward of my yielding.'

'You do me too much honour,' said Almona. 'Be so gracious

as to come to my chamber after sunset, as soon as the bright star Sheat appears above the horizon. You will find me upon a rose-coloured sofa, and you may do what you will with your servant.'

She then retired, taking with her his signature and leaving the old man a prey to desire and to misgivings about his strength. He spent the rest of the day bathing, and drank a cup of cinnamon from Ceylon infused with precious spices from Tidor and Ternate, while impatiently waiting for the star Sheat to rise.

Meanwhile the lovely Almona went to find the second patriarch. He assured her that the Sun, the Moon, and all the lights of the firmament were but will-o'-the-wisps in comparison with her charms. She begged the same favour, and was asked to pay the same price. She allowed herself to be persuaded, and made an assignation with the second patriarch at the rising of the star Algenib. Then she visited the third and the fourth priests, each time securing a signature and making an assignation at the rising of a star. She then went to request the judges to come to her chamber on important business. When they arrived, she showed them the four names and told them the price for which the priests had sold Zadig's ransom. Each of the four arrived at his appointed hour, and each, though much astonished to see his colleagues, was even more astonished to find the judges, before whom their shame was exposed. Zadig was saved. Setoc was so delighted with Almona's skill that he made her his wife. After throwing himself at the feet of his beautiful liberator, Zadig departed. Setoc and he were in tears as they said farewell; they vowed eternal friendship and promised each other that whichever was the first to make his fortune would share it with the other.

Zadig's way lay towards Syria. As he journeyed, he kept thinking of the unhappy Astarte and reflecting on the fate which persisted in teasing and persecuting him:

'Think of it!' he said to himself. 'Eighty ounces of gold

for not noticing a bitch! Condemned to be beheaded for
four bad verses in praise of the King! Nearly strangled because the Queen had some slippers the colour of my cap! Reduced to slavery for having rescued a woman from a beating!
And within an inch of burning for having saved the lives
of all the young widows in Arabia!'

CHAPTER 14

*

THE BRIGAND

On reaching the frontiers of Arabia and Syria, he passed by a pretty strong fortress, from which poured a number of Arabs, sword in hand. He found himself surrounded.

'All that you possess is ours,' cried one of them, 'and you belong to our master.'

Zadig's reply was to draw his sword, and his servant, who was a man of courage, did the same. They drove back and killed the first Arabs who set hands upon them. The numbers increased, but they showed no surprise and resolved to die fighting. It was two against a multitude: such a contest could not last long. The master of the fortress, whose name was Argobad, had been watching Zadig's prodigies of bravery from a window. He felt some respect for him, and hastened down in person to call off his people and deliver the two travellers.

'All that crosses my land is mine,' said he, 'as well as what I find on other people's. But you seem such a brave fellow that I exempt you from the common law.'

He bade him enter his fortress, and ordered his people to treat him well. In the evening Argobad decided to have supper with Zadig.

The lord of the fortress was one of those Arabs commonly called robbers; but amongst a heap of bad deeds, he sometimes did good ones. There were no limits to his greed for plunder, or to his generosity to others; he was fearless in action yet almost gentle when bargaining, debauched at table, yet merry in his debauches, and above all the soul of frankness. He took a great fancy to Zadig, whose conversation put him in good humour and spun out the meal. At last Argobad said to him:

'I advise you to enlist in my troop; you couldn't do better. It's not a bad trade, and one day you might become what I am.'

'May I ask you,' said Zadig, 'how long you have been following this noble profession?'

'From my earliest youth,' replied his lordship. 'I was manservant to an Arab; a clever fellow in his way, but my situation was unbearable. It vexed me to see that, though the earth belongs equally to all men, Fate had not kept me a corner in any part of it. I unburdened myself to an old Arab, who said to me: "My son, don't despair. Once upon a time there was a grain of sand which complained of being an atom lying disregarded in the desert; a few years went by, and it became a diamond; now it is the brightest jewel in the crown of the King of India." This story made a great impression on me; I was the grain of sand, I was determined to become a diamond. I began by stealing two horses; then I made up a party of companions to specialize in small caravans; and so little by little I put an end to that disproportion between myself and other men which I had begun with. I got my share of the good things of life, and recouped myself with interest, too. This made people respect me; I became a Master Brigand, and I took this castle by storm. The satrap of Syria wanted to turn me out; but I was already too rich to have anything to fear. I gave the satrap some money on condition that I kept the castle and enlarged my estates. He also made me Collector of Taxes in Northern Arabia for the King of Kings. I have taken good care to collect, and never to pay.

'The Grand Vizier of Babylon sent a little satrap here to strangle me in the name of King Moabdar. This fellow arrived with his instructions; but I had wind of everything: the four men whom he had brought to pull the noose I had throttled before his eyes, and I then asked what his commission to strangle me was worth to him. He told me his fees might amount to three hundred pieces of gold. I showed him that he had more to gain with me, and I made him an under-brigand. Today he is one of my best officers, and one of the richest, too. Believe me, you'll do as well as he did. The times have never been better for robbery, as Moabdar has been murdered, and all is confusion in Babylon.'

'Moabdar murdered!' cried Zadig. 'And what has happened to Queen Astarte?'

'I have no idea,' replied Argobad. 'All I know is that Moabdar went mad and has been murdered, that Babylon is a nest of cut-throats and the whole Empire is in ruins. There are still some fine chances for loot; in fact, I've done pretty well out of it myself already.'

'But what about the Queen?' said Zadig. 'Don't you know what has happened to the Queen? For heaven's sake tell me.'

'I have heard some talk of a Prince of Hyrcania,' he replied. 'She's probably one of his concubines, if she was not killed in the rioting. But I am more interested in booty than in news. I have captured several women in my raids, but I never keep any; I sell them for a good price if they are pretty, without inquiring what they are. No one pays for rank: a queen who happened to be ugly wouldn't find a customer. Perhaps I have sold Queen Astarte; perhaps she is dead; but it matters little to me, and I don't think you ought to care any more than I do.'

While he spoke, he had been drinking so generously that his mind became confused, and Zadig could not clearly discover anything more. He was dumbfounded, overwhelmed, and incapable of action. As for Argobad, he went on drinking and telling stories; he kept saying that he was the happiest of men, and urged Zadig to make himself equally happy. Overcome at last by the fumes of his wine, he fell into a peaceful sleep.

Zadig spent the night in violent perturbation.

'So the King went mad?' he kept saying, 'and was murdered? I can't help it, his fate drives me to tears! The

Empire is in ruins, and this brigand is happy! Such are the ways of Fortune! So this is Destiny! A robber happy, and the most lovely masterpiece of Nature perhaps barbarously destroyed, or alive in a state worse than death! Astarte, Astarte! What has become of you?'

At daybreak he questioned all whom he met in the castle, but everyone was busy, and no one would reply. New conquests had been made during the night, and the spoils were being divided. All he could obtain amidst the tumult was leave to depart. He took advantage of it without delay, and left the castle still in the depths of despair.

Zadig walked away in perturbation of spirit, his mind brooding upon the unfortunate Astarte, and the King of Babylon, and his faithful friend Cador, and the happy brigand Argobad, and that wanton whom the Babylonians had captured on the borders of Egypt, and in short upon all the unlucky accidents and misfortunes he had suffered.

CHAPTER 15

*

THE FISHERMAN

At a few leagues' distance from Argobad's castle he came to
a little river, and there he paused, still lamenting his destiny,
and looking upon himself as the very pattern of misfortune.
He noticed a fisherman lying on the bank. His net, to which
he scarcely paid attention, drooped languidly from his hand
as he raised his eyes to Heaven.

'I am undoubtedly the most unhappy of men,' the fisherman was saying. 'Time was when everyone agreed that I was
the most celebrated vendor of cream cheese in Babylon; and
now I am ruined. I had the prettiest wife that a man of my
condition could possess; and she has been false to me. I still
had a wretched hovel, and even that has been pillaged and
destroyed before my very eyes. My only shelter is a cabin;
my only means of subsistence is fishing, and I don't
catch any fish. This net of mine! What is the use
of casting it into the water any longer? I'll cast myself
instead.'

So saying he got up, and approached the river as if to hurl
himself in and end his life.

'Most remarkable!' said Zadig to himself. 'So there are men
just as wretched as I am!'

His impulse to save the fisherman's life was instinctive. He
ran towards him, checked him, and questioned him tenderly
and sympathetically. We fancy that we are less wretched
when we are not alone in our sufferings. But, according to
Zoroaster, that is the result not of evil destiny but of natural
laws; for we find ourselves attracted towards another's misfortunes, as like attracts like. The joy of a happy man would
be an insult to our misery; but two unhappy wretches are

like two weaks shrubs which lean upon each other and so resist the storm.

'Why do you yield to your troubles?' said Zadig to the fisherman.

'Because I see no help for it,' he replied. 'I was once the most respected man in the village of Derlback near Babylon, and with my wife's help I used to make the best cream cheese in the Empire. Queen Astarte, and Zadig the famous minister, were extremely fond of it. I had supplied their households with six hundred cheeses, and one day I went to town to be paid; but on reaching Babylon, I learned that the Queen and Zadig had disappeared. I ran to where Lord Zadig lived, though I had never seen him, and there I found the agents of the Supreme Council systematically pillaging his house in strict obedience to a legal warrant. I flew to the Queen's kitchens; some of those in charge told me she was dead, some said she was in prison, and others maintained that she had fled; but all assured me that no one would pay me for my cheeses. I went with my wife to call upon Lord Orcan, who was one of my customers, and to beg his protection in our misfortune. He agreed to protect my wife, but me he refused. She was whiter than the cream cheese from which my unhappiness arose. The brilliance of Tyrian purple was not more dazzling than the roses which enhanced the fairness of her skin. That was what determined Orcan to keep her and to turn me out of his house. I wrote my dear wife a letter in my distress.

' "Oh, yes!" she said to the bearer. "I know the man this letter is from. I have heard of him. They say he makes excellent cream cheese; please have some delivered, and see that he is paid."

'In my misfortune I decided to appeal to Justice. I had six ounces of gold left : two ounces had to be given to the solicitor I consulted, two to the barrister who undertook my case, and two to the Chief Justice's secretary. When all that was done, my case had not yet come up for hearing, and I had already spent more money than my cheeses and my wife were worth. I returned to my village intending to sell my house to get possession of my wife.

'My house was worth sixty ounces of gold, but it was obvious that I was poor and anxious to sell. The first man I approached offered me thirty ounces for it, the second offered me twenty, and the third ten. I was just about to settle in blind desperation when a Prince of Hyrcania marched on Babylon, destroying everything in his way. My house was first pillaged and then burnt to the ground.

'Having thus lost my money, my wife, and my house, I withdrew to this region where you now see me. I have tried to make a living as a fisherman, but the fish mock me just as men do. I catch nothing, and I am dying of hunger. But for your noble sympathy, I should have perished in the river.'

The fisherman did not tell this story without interruption, for Zadig kept breaking in with great agitation:

'Then you know nothing of the Queen's fate?'

'No, my lord,' the fisherman would reply. 'But I know that the Queen and Zadig never paid me for my cream cheeses, that I have been robbed of my wife, and that I am in despair.'

'I am pretty sure,' said Zadig, 'that you will not lose all your money. I have heard of this Zadig; he's an honest man; and if he returns to Babylon, as he hopes, he will give you more than he owes you. But as for your wife, she's not so honest. I recommend you not to try to recover her. Take my advice, and go to Babylon; I shall be there before you because I am on horseback, and you are on foot. Seek audience of the noble Cador; tell him that you have met his friend, and wait for me at his house. Be off now; perhaps you won't always be unhappy.'

'All-powerful Ormuzd!' he continued, 'you call on me to console this man, but on whom will you call to console *me*?'

With these words, he gave the fisherman half the money he had brought from Arabia; and the fisherman, in astonishment and delight, kissed the feet of Cador's friend, and said:

'You are an angel sent to save me!'

Zadig, however, kept asking for news, and shedding tears.

'How is this, my lord?' exclaimed the fisherman. 'Can it be that you are just as unhappy, you who do so much good?'

'A hundred times more unhappy than you are,' replied Zadig.

'But how can it be,' said the worthy fellow, 'that the man who gives should be in greater need of pity than the man who receives?'

'It's because your greatest misfortune is mere want,' replied Zadig, 'whereas my unhappiness is at my heart.'

'Can it be that Orcan has run off with your wife?' asked the fisherman.

The question recalled to Zadig's mind all his adventures, and he ran over the list of his misfortunes beginning with the Queen's bitch till his arrival at Argobad's castle.

'Yes,' said he to the fisherman, 'Orcan deserves punishing; but it is usually such men who are Fortune's favourites. However, go to Lord Cador's and wait for me.'

They then parted company. The fisherman walked away thanking his stars, and Zadig ran off cursing his.

CHAPTER 16

*

THE COCKATRICE

HE came to a beautiful meadow, and there he saw several women looking for something with absorbed attention. He took the liberty of approaching one of them, and asked whether he might have the honour of helping them in their search.

'Take care you don't,' replied the Syrian woman. 'What we are looking for can only be touched by women.'

'How very strange!' said Zadig. 'Dare I beg you to tell me what it is that only women are allowed to touch?'

'It's a cockatrice,' she said.

'A cockatrice, Madam? And may I ask why you are looking for a cockatrice?'

'It's for Ogul, our lord and master, whose castle you see on the banks of that river at the bottom of the meadow. We are his humble slaves. Lord Ogul is ill; his doctor has ordered him to eat a cockatrice cooked in rose-water; and as it is a very rare creature, which never lets itself be caught except by women, Lord Ogul has promised to take as his beloved wife the one that brings him a cockatrice. Let me go on looking, if you please; for you see what I should lose if the others should steal a march on me.'

Zadig left the Syrian woman and her companions searching for their cockatrice, and resumed his way through the meadow. On the bank of a little stream he found another lady, seated on the grass, who was not searching for anything; she seemed of noble bearing, although her face was hidden by a veil. She was leaning over the stream, and deep sighs kept breaking from her lips. In her hand she held a little stick with which she was tracing letters in the fine sand which lay between the grass and the stream. Zadig was curious to see what this woman was writing. He drew near, and saw to his surprise the letter z and then an A; a D followed, and he started with excitement. Never was anyone so astonished as he when he saw the last two letters of his own name. He stood transfixed for some moments; then, breaking the silence, with faltering voice he said:

'Forgive a stranger in misfortune, noble lady, for daring to ask you by what amazing chance I find the name of Zadig here, traced by your divine hand?'

His voice and the words he uttered roused the lady. Lifting her veil with a trembling hand, she looked at Zadig, and uttering a tender cry of joy mingled with surprise, she yielded to all the varied emotions which beset her and fell fainting into his arms. It was Astarte herself, the Queen of Babylon whom Zadig both adored and reproached himself for adoring; it was she for whom he had shed so many tears, and for whose fate he had been so deeply concerned. For a moment he felt stunned; and when he once more fixed his gaze upon Astarte's eyes, which opened with a confused yet tender look of weariness, he cried aloud:

'Ye Immortal Powers, who preside over the destinies of frail humanity, can it be that you have restored Astarte to me? Or am I dreaming the moment, the place, the very state in which I see her?'

He threw himself upon his knees before Astarte, and prostrated himself in the dust at her feet. The Queen of Babylon raised him up, and made him sit beside her on the bank of the stream; more than once she wiped away the tears from his eyes. Twenty times she tried to speak, but was constantly interrupted by his sighs. She questioned him on the happy chance which had reunited them, but repeatedly broke in on his replies with further questions. She began to tell him about her misfortunes, and then desired to hear of his. When at last they had both quietened the transport of their feelings,

Zadig related to her in a few words how he came to be in the meadow.

'But how is it,' he continued, 'that I find my unfortunate and revered Queen in this lonely place, dressed as a slave, and in the company of other slaves who are searching for a cockatrice to be cooked in rose-water on a doctor's prescription?'

'While they are searching for their cockatrice,' said the beautiful Astarte, 'I will tell you all that I have suffered, for all of which I forgive the heavenly powers now that I see you once more. You know that the King my husband disliked you for being the most agreeable of men; and that was why he resolved one night to have you strangled and me poisoned. You know how Heaven allowed my little dumb servant to warn me of the orders of His Supreme Majesty. The faithful Cador had scarcely compelled you to obey me and depart, when he ventured to enter my apartments by a secret entrance at dead of night. He carried me off and led me to the Temple of Ormuzd, where the priest his brother hid me in that huge statue whose base touches the foundations of the Temple and whose head reaches the roof. It was as though I were buried alive there, but I was attended by the priest, and I lacked nothing that was necessary. Meanwhile at daybreak His Majesty's apothecary entered my bedchamber with a potion of henbane, opium, hemlock, black hellebore, and aconite; and another officer went to your house with a noose of blue silk. There was no one to be found. To deceive the King more successfully, Cador pretended to come and accuse us both. He said that you had gone towards India and that I had set out in the direction of Memphis; assassins were accordingly sent after both of us.

'The messengers who were looking for me did not know me by sight. I had scarcely ever unveiled myself, except only to you, in the presence of my husband and at his orders. They went off in pursuit of me with a sketch of my appearance which had been made for them. A woman of the same height, and perhaps with greater charms, was noticed on the frontiers of Egypt; she was wandering about in tears. Having no doubt that this woman was the Queen of Babylon, they brought her to Moabdar. The first effect of their mistake was to put the King into a violent rage; but on a closer inspection of the woman, he found her decidedly beautiful and was appeased. She was called Missouf. I have since been told that in the Egyptian language her name means "the pretty wanton". That was what she turned out to be. But with all her whims, she was clever too, and she captivated Moabdar and inveigled him into making her his wife. From that moment her character was completely revealed, and she recklessly indulged all the most foolish whims she could think of. She determined that the Chief Mage should dance before her, though he was old and troubled with the gout; and when he refused, she persecuted him outrageously. She commanded her Master of the Horse to make her a jam tart. It was no good for the Master of the Horse to point out that he wasn't a pastrycook; he had to make the tart; and he was dismissed because it was overcooked. She gave the office of Master of the Horse to her dwarf, and the post of Chancellor to a page. That was how she governed Babylon. Everyone missed me. The King, who had been a kindly man until he decided to have me poisoned and you strangled, seemed to have lost all sense of duty in his overwhelming love for the pretty wanton. He came to the Temple at the festival of the sacred flame. I saw him implore the Gods for Missouf at the feet of the statue where I was concealed; I lifted up my voice and cried to him : "The Gods reject the vows of a King turned tyrant, who has plotted the death of a sensible wife to marry a madcap!" Moabdar was so dumbfounded at these words that his mind became disordered. The oracle that I had uttered and the tyranny practised by Missouf deprived him of his reason; he went mad a few days later.

'His madness, which seemed a punishment from Heaven, was the signal for revolt. The people rose in insurrection and rushed to arms. Babylon, which had so long been steeped in effeminate idleness, became the scene of a terrible civil war. I was taken from the hollow of my statue and set at the head of a faction. Cador hurried to Memphis to bring you back to Babylon. The Prince of Hyrcania heard the melancholy news and came with his army to make a third faction in Chaldea. He attacked the King, who fled before him with his madcap Egyptian. Moabdar died of the wounds he received, and Missouf fell into the hands of the conqueror.

'It was my misfortune to be captured by a detachment of Hyrcanians and led before the Prince at the very same time as Missouf was brought into his presence. You will no doubt be pleased to learn that the Prince found me more beautiful than the Egyptian; but you will be vexed to hear that he consigned me to his harem. He boldly informed me that, when he had completed a military expedition on which he was engaged, he would come back to me. You can imagine my grief. The ties which bound me to Moabdar were broken, I was free to be Zadig's, but I was in the power of a barbarian. I answered him with all the loftiness of my rank and feelings. I had always heard that Heaven invests the nobly-born with an air of grandeur which, at a word or a look, can humble any rash creatures who dare show the least disrespect. I spoke as a Queen; but I was treated as a handmaid. The Hyrcanian did not even deign to answer me, but said to his black eunuch that, though I was pert, he thought I was pretty; and he ordered him to take care of me and put me on the same diet as his favourite mistresses so as to improve my complexion and make me worthy of his favours at such time as he chose to honour me with them. I told him I would rather die. He laughingly replied that he was used to such expressions – people did not take their lives; and he left me as casually as a man who has just added a parrot to his collection. What a situation for the most noble queen in the whole world, and, I will add, for the heart which belonged to Zadig!'

At these words he threw himself at her feet, and bathed

them with his tears. Astarte tenderly raised him, and continued in these words:

'I saw that I was in the power of a barbarian, and the rival of a fool with whom I was imprisoned. She told me the story of her adventures in Egypt. I decided from the way she described you, the time, the dromedary you were riding, and from all the circumstances, that it was indeed Zadig who had fought for her. I have no doubt that you were at Memphis, and I determined to get there. "Lovely Missouf," said I, "you are much more amusing than I am; you will afford the Prince of Hyrcania much more diversion than I can. Help me to escape, and you will reign alone. You will make me happy, while you rid yourself of a rival." Missouf arranged with me how I was to escape, and I departed secretly with an Egyptian slave.

'I had almost reached Arabia, when a notorious brigand called Argobad carried me off and sold me to some merchants, who brought me to this castle where Lord Ogul lives. He bought me without knowing who I was. This Ogul is given up to sensuality. His only interest is in gross living, and he believes that God sent him into the world for nothing but the pleasures of the table. He is so extremely corpulent as to be always in danger of suffocation. His doctor has little authority over him when his digestion is working, but rules him despotically when he has eaten too much. He has persuaded him that he could cure him with a cockatrice cooked in rose-water. Lord Ogul has promised to marry whichever one of his slaves brings him a cockatrice. You notice that I am unconcerned at their eager contest for this honour. I never had less desire to find this cockatrice than since Heaven has permitted me to see you once more.'

Astarte and Zadig then gave expression to everything that feelings so long restrained, everything that misfortune and love, could inspire in the noblest and most impassioned breasts; and the spirits which preside over human love carried their words up to the crystal sphere of Venus.

The women returned to Ogul's castle without finding anything. Zadig presented himself, and spoke to Ogul in these words:

'May everlasting Health descend from heaven to take you under her care! I am a doctor. I made haste to come here when I heard of your illness, and I have brought you a cockatrice cooked in rose-water. I don't aspire to marry you. All I ask is freedom for a young slave from Babylon whom you have had for several days; and I consent to remain in slavery in her place, if I do not have the good fortune to cure Lord Ogul the Magnificent.'

The proposal was accepted. Astarte left for Babylon with Zadig's servant, and promised to send a messenger frequently to inform him of everything that happened. Their farewells were as tender as their reunion had been. The moment of reunion and the moment of separation are the two greatest crises of life; so it is written in the Great Book of Zend. Zadig loved the Queen as much as he protested, and the Queen loved Zadig more than she acknowledged.

Zadig then spoke to Ogul as follows:

'My lord, my cockatrice is not to be eaten. Its healing quality must enter your body through the pores. I have placed it in a little bladder which has been inflated and covered with a fine skin. You must strike this bladder with all your might, and I will send it back to you repeatedly; a few days of this treatment will show you what my skill can do.'

The first day Ogul was quite out of breath, and thought he would die of fatigue. The second day he was less tired, and slept better. In a week he recovered all the strength, health, nimbleness, and gaiety of his most robust years.

'You have played with a balloon, and you have been moderate in your food,' said Zadig. 'Understand that there is no such thing as a cockatrice, and that a man can always keep well with moderation and exercise. Good health and intemperance cannot subsist together. The idea is as fantastic as the philosophers' stone, or astrology, or the theology of the mages.'

Ogul's principal physician recognized that here was a man dangerous to the interests of medicine, so he plotted with the apothecary to send Zadig to look for cockatrices in the other world. Thus, having always been punished for well-doing, he was on the point of destruction for having cured a noble glutton. He was invited to an excellent dinner, and was to have been poisoned during the second course; but during the first he received a message from Astarte, at which he left the table and departed. When a man is loved by a beautiful woman, said the great Zoroaster, he always gets out of trouble.

CHAPTER 17

*

THE TOURNAMENT

THE Queen had been received in Babylon with the enthusiasm always shown to a beautiful princess who has been unhappy. Babylon now seemed to be more peaceful. The Prince of Hyrcania had been killed in a fight, and the victorious Babylonians declared that Astarte should marry whoever was chosen as sovereign. No one wanted the most important position in the world, that of Astarte's husband and King of Babylon, to depend upon intrigue and faction; and all swore to acknowledge as king the man possessed of the greatest wisdom and the greatest valour. A huge tiltyard was made a few miles from the town, and was surrounded by amphitheatres magnificently decorated. Here the combatants were to repair in full armour. Behind the amphitheatres each was to have a separate apartment where he could be neither seen nor recognized by anyone. Each combatant had to encounter four knights. Those who were lucky enough to conquer all four were then to joust with each other, so that whoever was left master of the field should be proclaimed victor of the tournament. He must then return four days later with the same arms and solve the riddles propounded by the mages. If he did not solve the riddles, he did not become king, and the tournament was to be resumed until a man was found triumphant in both these contests; for they were absolutely determined to have as king the wisest of men as well as the most valiant. The Queen meanwhile was to be strictly guarded. Her face covered by a veil, she was to be allowed only to watch the games but not to speak to any of the claimants, so that there should be neither favour nor injustice.

That was what Astarte made known to her lover in the hope that he would show for her more valour and wit than any other man. He departed with a prayer to Venus to fortify his courage and clarify his wit, and reached the banks of the Euphrates on the eve of this great day. He had his device inscribed with those of the other combatants but concealed his face and name, as the law decreed. He then went to rest himself in the apartment which fell to him by lot. His friend Cador, who had returned to Babylon after fruitlessly searching for him in Egypt, had a complete suit of armour conveyed to his room from the Queen. He also sent him on his own behalf the finest horse in Persia. Zadig recognized the hand of Astarte in these presents, and from them his courage and his love derived new strength and new hope.

The following day, when the Queen had taken her place under a jewelled canopy and the amphitheatres were filled with all the ladies and all the ranks of Babylon, the combatants appeared in the arena. Each proceeded to place his device at the feet of the Archimage. The devices were drawn by lots, and Zadig's was drawn last. The first to advance was a wealthy nobleman called Itobad, who was inordinately vain, rather timid, very clumsy, and stupid. His servants had persuaded him that such a man as he ought to be king, and he was in complete agreement. He was therefore resplendent from head to foot in a suit of gold enamelled with green; his plume was green, and his lance was decked with green ribbons. It was clear from the way Itobad managed his horse that it was not for such a man as he that Heaven had destined the sceptre of Babylon. The first knight to charge unsaddled him, and the second overturned him on the buttocks of his horse with his legs in the air and his arms extended. Itobad recovered himself, but in such an awkward way as to set the whole amphitheatre laughing. The third knight did not condescend to use his lance, but made a thrust at him and caught him by the right leg, made him turn about, and brought him tumbling on to the sand. The attendant squires ran up to him laughing, and put him back in his saddle. The fourth knight took him by the left leg and sent him flying on the other side. He was led back amid scornful shouts to his apartment, where by law he had to pass the night. As he hobbled along he said to himself: 'What an unlucky accident for such a man as I.'

The other knights acquitted themselves better. Some overcame two combatants in succession, some as many as three. Only Prince Otames vanquished four. At last it was Zadig's turn to fight. He unhorsed four knights in succession with all possible skill. Thus it only remained to be seen whether Otames or Zadig was the victor. Otames was wearing blue and gold armour with a plume of the same colours; Zadig's armour was white. The supporters of the Blue and the White Knights were equally divided; but the Queen, whose heart was fluttering in anxiety, offered prayers to Heaven for a white victory.

The two champions made such dexterous thrusts and turns, they wielded their lances so skilfully and sat so firmly in the saddle, that everyone except the Queen wished that there could be two kings in Babylon. But at last, when their horses were tired and their lances broken, Zadig made a clever stroke. Passing behind the Blue Knight, he hurled himself upon the horse's buttocks, and seizing his opponent round the waist he threw him to the earth; then, jumping into the saddle in his place, he wheeled round Otames, who lay stretched upon the ground.

The whole amphitheatre cried, 'The White Knight has won!'

Otames, indignant, got up and drew his sword; at this Zadig leapt from his horse, sabre in hand. They then engaged in a new fight on the arena, with strength and skill triumphing turn and turn about. The plumes of their helmets, the bolts of their arm-guards, the very links of their chain mail leapt far and wide under the numberless blows which were rained upon them. They struck with point and with edge, now on the right side, now on the left, now at the head, and now at the breast; now they gave way, now they advanced; now they measured swords, now they closed in and seized each other; they twisted like serpents and attacked like lions. Sparks flew at every blow they struck. At last when Zadig had momentarily paused to recover, he stopped and made a feint; then, thrusting at Otames, he brought him down and disarmed him.

At this, Otames exclaimed: 'White Knight! You are the man to reign over Babylon!'

The Queen was in an ecstasy of joy. The Blue Knight and the White Knight were each led back to his apartment as the law prescribed, just as all the other combatants had been. There they were attended by dumb servants, who brought them food to eat – perhaps it was the Queen's little dumb servant who tended Zadig. They were then left by themselves to sleep till the following morning, when the victor was to present his device to the Archimage and to reveal his identity.

So tired was Zadig that he slept well in spite of being in love. Itobad, who lay near him, did not sleep at all. He got up during the night and went into Zadig's apartment, took the white armour with Zadig's device, and put his own green armour in its place. At daybreak he strode proudly before the Archimage and declared that he was the victor, even such a man as he. This was unexpected; nevertheless he was proclaimed while Zadig was still asleep. Astarte was amazed and returned to Babylon in the depths of despair.

The amphitheatre was already nearly empty when Zadig awoke. He searched for his arms, and could find only the green suit, but he was obliged to dress himself in it, as he had nothing else at hand. His indignation and astonishment can be imagined as he angrily put on this costume and sallied forth in it.

Those who were still in the amphitheatre and the arena all greeted him with jeers. He was surrounded and insulted to his face; never had a man to bear such gross humiliation. His patience gave way, and with a few strokes of his sabre he scattered the crowd who had presumed to affront him; but he did not know what course to take. He could not visit the Queen; he could not reclaim the white armour she had sent him, for that would have compromised her. Thus, while she was overcome with grief, he was in a state of fury and disquiet. He walked along the banks of the Euphrates, revolving in his mind all the disgraces he had suffered, from the time of the woman who hated one-eyed men down to this adventure with his armour, and he persuaded himself that his evil star had destined him to be unhappy and that there was no help for it.

'That's what comes of waking up too late,' said he. 'If I had not slept so well, I should be King of Babylon, and Astarte would be mine. Learning, virtue, and courage have only brought me misfortune.'

A murmur against Providence at last escaped him, and he was tempted to believe that all is governed by a cruel Destiny which persecutes good men and befriends knights in green. One source of vexation was wearing the green armour which had brought him so many insults. He sold it for less than it was worth to a merchant passing by and obtained from him a simple dress and hat. Thus arrayed, he wandered beside the Euphrates in deep despair, secretly accusing Providence of always persecuting him.

CHAPTER 18

✦

THE HERMIT

As he walked along, he met a hermit whose white and venerable beard reached down to his girdle. In his hand he held
a book, which he was reading attentively. Zadig stopped and
made him a low bow, at which the hermit greeted him so
mildly and graciously that Zadig was impelled to talk to him
and ask him what book he was reading.

'It is the Book of Destinies,' said the hermit. 'Would you
like to look at it?'

He placed the book in Zadig's hands; but although he
knew several languages, Zadig was unable to decipher a
single letter of it, which increased his curiosity still more.

'You seem greatly troubled,' said the worthy Father.

'Alas! I have good reason to be!' said Zadig.

'If you will allow me to accompany you,' replied the old
man, 'perhaps I may be useful to you. I have sometimes
afforded consolation to an unhappy spirit.'

The hermit's manner, his beard, and his book all aroused
Zadig's respect. He found himself conversing with a superior
intelligence, for the hermit spoke of Destiny, Justice,
Morality, Sovereign Good, Human Frailty, Virtue, and Vice
with such lively and affecting eloquence that Zadig felt
drawn towards him by an irresistible charm, and earnestly
begged him not to leave him until they returned to Babylon.

'And I,' said the old man, 'have a favour to ask of you:
swear by Ormuzd that for a few days you will not leave me
whatever I may do.'

Zadig swore it, and they set off together.

That evening the two travellers arrived at a magnificent
castle, where the hermit begged hospitality for himself and

the young man who accompanied him. The porter, who might have been taken for a great nobleman, showed them in with a sort of disdainful kindness. They were handed over to a principal servant, who conducted them round his master's magnificent rooms and then ushered them to the lower end of his table, without the lord of the castle honouring them with a glance; but like the others they were served with delicacy and profusion. They were then offered a golden basin studded with emeralds and rubies to wash in, and were taken to a beautiful bedroom to rest. Next morning a servant brought them each a piece of gold and dismissed them.

'The master of the house,' said Zadig, as they walked along, 'seemed a bountiful man, even if a little proud. He has a noble idea of hospitality.'

As he said these words, he noticed that a kind of knapsack which the hermit carried bulged suspiciously, and inside it he saw the golden basin studded with jewels, which the hermit had stolen. He did not dare to draw attention to it, but he felt greatly surprised.

Towards midday the hermit knocked at the door of a mean little house where a rich miser lived, and asked for a few hours' hospitality. An old servant in tattered dress gave him a surly reception and showed the hermit and Zadig into a stable, where they were given a few rotten olives to eat, with some stale bread and flat beer. The hermit ate and drank with as much contentment as he had shown the previous evening; then, turning to the old servant, who was watching them to see that they stole nothing and kept urging them to leave, he gave him the two pieces of gold he had received in the morning and thanked him for all his attention to their needs.

'Be so good,' he added, 'as to let me speak to your master.'

The old servant was astonished at this request, but he took the two travellers and introduced them.

'My noble lord,' said the hermit, 'I can only give Your Grace the most humble thanks for the manner in which you have received us. Pray condescend to accept this golden basin as a humble token of my gratitude.'

The miser nearly fell backwards with surprise; but without waiting for him to recover from his astonishment, the hermit quickly departed with his young companion.

'Father,' said Zadig, 'I can scarcely believe my senses. You don't seem to behave at all like other men: you steal a golden basin studded with jewels from a nobleman who has entertained you magnificently, and you give it to a miser who has treated you with disrespect.'

'My son,' replied the hermit, 'that grandee only entertains strangers out of vanity, to have his riches admired. He will become a wiser man, and the miser will learn to practise hospitality. Don't let anything surprise you, and follow me.'

Zadig still did not know whether he was dealing with the most foolish or the wisest of men; but the hermit spoke with such authority that Zadig, who was bound by his promise moreover, could not refrain from following him.

That evening they came to a delightful house, built in a charming yet simple style, with no suggestion of meanness nor yet of prodigality. The owner was a sage who had retired from the world to study wisdom and virtue undisturbed, a pursuit of which he never wearied. He had taken delight in building himself this retreat, where he used to entertain strangers liberally yet without ostentation. He first led the two travellers himself to a comfortable room where he made them rest, then came himself some little time later to invite them to an elegant meal, at which he discreetly talked about the latest revolutions in Babylon. He professed sincere attachment to the Queen, and wished that Zadig had appeared in the lists to compete for the crown; 'but', he added, 'men don't deserve a king like Zadig'; at which Zadig blushed, and his griefs were renewed. They all agreed that things do not always happen in this world as the wisest men would like; but the hermit maintained that no one knows the ways of Providence, and that men were wrong to pass judgement on a whole of which they perceive only the smallest part.

They talked of the passions.

'How disastrous they are!' said Zadig.

'No,' said the hermit, 'they are the winds which fill the sails of the ship. They overwhelm it sometimes; but without them it could not sail. Bile makes us sick and angry, but without bile we could not live. Everything in this life is dangerous, but everything is necessary.'

They talked of pleasure, and the hermit proved that it is a gift of God; for, said he, man cannot give himself either sensations or ideas: he receives them both. Pain and pleasure descend upon him from elsewhere, like his own being.

Zadig marvelled that a man could reason so well who had acted so oddly. At last, after conversation which had been both instructive and agreeable, their host led the two travellers to their room once more, and gave thanks to Heaven for having sent him two men so wise and virtuous. He offered them money so courteously that it would have been impossible to take offence; but the hermit refused to accept it, and said that he would take leave of him, as he intended to set out for Babylon before daybreak. They bade each other an affectionate farewell, Zadig in particular feeling both admiration and attachment for so worthy a man.

When the hermit and he were alone in their room, they had much to say to each other in praise of their host. At daybreak the old man roused his companion.

'It is time for us to be away,' he said. 'But while everyone is still asleep, I want to leave this man a testimony of my esteem and affection.'

With these words, he took a torch and set fire to the house.

Zadig cried aloud in horror, and tried to prevent such a dreadful deed; but the hermit carried him off by superior force, and the house was left ablaze. When they had gone some distance from the scene, the hermit turned round and calmly watched the house burning.

'Thank God for that!' he said. 'The house of my dear host is completely destroyed from top to bottom. He's a lucky man!'

At this Zadig was tempted to burst out laughing and abuse the reverend father, and then to thrash him and run away; but he did none of these things, for the hermit had gained such an ascendancy over him that he was constrained to follow him to a night's lodging for the last time.

They stayed with a virtuous and charitable widow, who had a nephew of fourteen, a boy full of good qualities and her only hope. She did the honours of her house as best she could, and next morning she told her nephew to accompany the travellers as far as a bridge which had recently been broken and where the river-crossing was dangerous in consequence. The boy readily obeyed, and walked in front of them.

When they were crossing the bridge, the hermit said to the boy: 'Come here. I must show my gratitude to your aunt.'

He then took him by the hair, and threw him into the river. The child fell, and reappeared for a moment above the water before being swallowed up in the torrent.

'You monster!' cried Zadig. 'You most abandoned villain!'

'You promised me to have more patience,' said the hermit, interrupting him. 'Let me tell you that under the ruins of that house which Providence set on fire, the master has found immense treasure. And that boy whose neck Providence has wrung would have murdered his aunt within a year, and would have murdered you a year later.'

'Who told you so, you wretch?' cried Zadig. 'And even if you read the event in that Book of Destinies of yours, who has given you permission, I should like to know, to drown a child that has done you no harm?'

As the Babylonian was speaking, he noticed that the old man no longer had a beard, and that his face was taking on the features of youth. His hermit's garb disappeared, and four beautiful wings covered a body resplendent in majesty and light.

'Heavenly messenger!' cried Zadig, as he prostrated himself, 'Angel of God! Now I see that you have descended from the Empyrean to teach a weak mortal to submit to the eternal edicts!'

'Men judge everything,' said the Angel Jesrad, 'without understanding anything. Of all men it was you who most deserved enlightenment.'

Zadig asked permission to speak. 'I distrust my judgement,' said he. 'But I have one doubt, and I must humbly beg you to resolve it: would it not have been better to correct that child and make him virtuous instead of drowning him?'

Jesrad replied: 'If he had been virtuous and had lived, he was destined to be murdered himself, with the wife he was to marry and the child he was to have by her.'

'But must there always be crime and misfortune?' said Zadig. 'Must misfortune always befall the good?'

'Evildoers,' replied Jesrad, 'are always unhappy. They serve to test the small number of just men scattered over the Earth, and there is no evil which does not give rise to good.'

'But supposing,' said Zadig, 'there were no evil, and there were only good?'

'Then,' replied Jesrad, 'this world would be another world. The sequence of events would show another order of wisdom; and that other order, which would be perfect, can exist only in the eternal dwelling-place of the Supreme Being, whom evil cannot approach. He has created millions of worlds, each entirely unlike the rest. This immense variety is an attribute of his immense power. There are no two leaves of all the trees upon the earth, no two stars in the infinite fields of heaven, which are alike; and all that you see on this little atom where you were born must be fixed in its place and time according to the immutable decrees of him who encompasses all. Men think that this child who has just died fell into the water by accident, and that by such another accident the house was burned; but there is no such thing as accident. All is either trial or punishment, reward or foresight. Remember that fisherman who thought himself the most unhappy of men. Ormuzd sent you to change his destiny. You are a weak mortal, and have no business to argue about what you must adore.'

'But –' said Zadig.

As he said the word, the Angel took flight towards the Empyrean. Zadig fell on his knees, worshipping Providence in true submissiveness. The Angel called to him from high up in the air:

'Make your way towards Babylon.'

CHAPTER 19

*

THE RIDDLES

ZADIG was beside himself, and walked at random, like a man who has narrowly escaped a thunderbolt. He entered Babylon on the day when those who had fought in the lists were already assembled in the great hall of the palace to solve the riddles and reply to questions from the Archimage. All the knights had arrived except Green Armour. As soon as Zadig appeared in the city, people gathered round; their eyes could not tire of looking at him or their lips of blessing him, and there was scarce a heart that did not wish the empire his. Green Eyes saw him pass and turned aside with a shudder, but the people carried him to the place of assembly. The Queen, who had been informed of his arrival, was in a tumult of hope and fear. She was a prey to anxiety, and could understand neither why Zadig was unarmed nor how Itobad had come to wear the white armour. A confused murmur arose at the sight of Zadig. There was surprise and pleasure at seeing him again; but only knights who had fought were allowed to appear in the assembly.

'I fought like anyone else,' said he. 'But there is someone else here bearing my colours; and while awaiting the honour of proving it, I ask permission to be present for the solving of the riddles.'

A vote was taken; his reputation for uprightness was still so forcibly impressed on everyone's mind that there was no hesitation in admitting him.

The Archimage first put the following question: 'Of all things in the world, what is it which is both the longest and the shortest, the quickest and the slowest, the most divisible and the most extensive, the most neglected and the most re-

99

gretted, without which nothing can be done, which consumes all that is little, and gives life to all that is great?'

It was Itobad's turn to speak first. He replied that such a man as he knew nothing about riddles; it was enough for him to have conquered by force of arms. Some said the answer to the riddle was Fortune; some said the Earth; some said Light. Zadig said it was Time.

'Nothing is longer,' he added, 'for it is the measure of Eternity; yet nothing is shorter, for there is not enough for all that we would like to do. Nothing is slower for him that waits, and nothing more swift for him that enjoys. It reaches infinite greatness, and can be divided into infinite smallness. All men neglect it, yet all regret its loss; and nothing is done without it. It causes all that is unworthy of posterity to be forgotten, and it immortalizes deeds that are great.'

The assembly agreed that Zadig was right.

The next question was as follows: 'What is it that we receive without thanks and enjoy without understanding, that we give to others in moments of ecstasy, and lose without perceiving the fact?'

Each gave his answer, but Zadig alone guessed that it was Life; and he solved the other riddles with the same ease. Itobad kept saying that nothing was easier, and that he could have managed it just as readily if he had cared to take the trouble. Questions were put on the subjects of justice, sovereign good, and the art of government. Zadig's replies were considered to be the soundest. It's a great pity, people said, that so good a wit should be so bad a knight.

'Noble lords,' said Zadig, 'I had the honour to be the victor in the lists! The white armour belongs to me. Lord Itobad seized it from me while I slept, apparently thinking it would suit him better than the green. I am ready to prove to him here and now before your eyes, wearing only my gown and sword against all the beautiful white armour he has taken from me, that it was I who had the honour of conquering the brave Otames!'

Itobad accepted the challenge with the greatest confidence. He never doubted that, with helmet, breastplates, and arm-guards, he could easily overcome a champion in gown and nightcap. Zadig drew his sword and saluted the Queen, who looked at him, overcome with joy and fear. Itobad drew his without saluting anyone. He approached Zadig as though he had nothing to fear, and made ready to cleave his head. Zadig knew how to parry the blow by opposing the hilt of his sword to the point of his adversary's in such a way that Itobad's sword was broken. Then, seizing his enemy round the body, Zadig threw him to the ground, and offering the point of his sword to the joint of his breastplate, he said: 'Lay down your arms, or I kill you.'

Itobad submitted, surprised as usual at the disgraces that happened to such a man as he, and Zadig calmly stripped him of his magnificent helmet, his superb breastplate, his beautiful arm-guards, and his shining cuisses. Clothing himself in them, he threw himself at the feet of Astarte.

Cador easily proved that the armour belonged to Zadig. He was recognized as King by unanimous consent, more particularly by Astarte, who enjoyed the pleasure, after so many adversities, of seeing her lover proved worthy to be her husband in the eyes of the whole world. Itobad returned home to be called 'Your Highness', and Zadig became King and a happy man. He recalled what the Angel Jesrad had told him, and he even remembered the grain of sand that became a diamond. The Queen and he worshipped Providence.

Zadig allowed Missouf the pretty wanton to travel abroad. He sent for the robber Argobad, and gave him an honourable rank in his army, promising to promote him to the highest posts if he behaved like a true soldier, and to hang him if he returned to brigandage.

Setoc was recalled from farthest Arabia, with the beautiful Almona, to be chief minister of trade in Babylon. Cador received the rank and the affection which his services deserved; he was the friend of the King, and the King was thus the only monarch in the world to have a friend. The little dumb servant was not forgotten. The fisherman was given a beautiful house, and Orcan was ordered to pay him a large sum and give him back his wife; but the fisherman had learned wisdom, and took only the money.

The beautiful Semira could not console herself for believing that Zadig would lose an eye, and Azora did not cease to lament that she had wanted to cut off his nose. He calmed their grief with presents. Green Eyes died of rage and shame. The Empire enjoyed peace, glory, and abundance, for it was governed by justice and by love. This was the happiest age of the world. All gave thanks to Zadig, and Zadig gave thanks to Heaven.

L'INGÉNU
(THE CHILD OF NATURE)

A TRUE STORY TAKEN FROM
THE MANUSCRIPTS OF
FATHER QUESNEL

CHAPTER I

*

HOW THE PRIOR OF OUR LADY OF THE
MOUNTAIN AND HIS SISTER MET
A HURON INDIAN

ONE day long ago St Dunstan, who was Irish by nationality
and a saint by profession, set sail from Ireland for the coast
of France on a little mountain, which deposited him in St
Malo bay. On landing, he pronounced a blessing upon his
mountain, which made him a low bow and returned to
Ireland by the same route it had followed in coming.

Dunstan founded a little priory near by and called it the
Priory of the Mountain, a name it still bears, as everybody
knows.

In the evening of the 15th of July 1689, the Abbé de Kerkabon, Prior of Our Lady of the Mountain, was taking a walk
by the seashore with Mademoiselle de Kerkabon, his sister,
to enjoy the fresh air. The Prior, who was getting on in years,
was an excellent churchman; he was now as much beloved
by his neighbours as he had formerly been by his neighbours'
wives. What made him particularly respected was that he was
the only clergyman in the district who did not have to be
carried to bed after dining with his colleagues. He had a
decent knowledge of theology; and when he was tired of
reading St Augustine, he turned for amusement to Rabelais.
And so everyone spoke well of him.

Mademoiselle de Kerkabon still kept her looks at the age
of forty-five. Though she had had a great mind to marry, she
had never found a husband. She was a good-natured woman,
warm-hearted, fond of pleasure, and spiritually-minded.

As the Prior looked at the sea, he remarked to his sister
with a sigh: 'It was from this very spot that our poor brother

set sail in the frigate *Swallow* in 1669 to go and serve in Canada, and took with him his wife, our dear sister-in-law, Madame de Kerkabon. If he had not been killed, we might still hope to see him again.'

'Do you believe,' said Mademoiselle de Kerkabon, 'that our sister-in-law was really eaten by the Iroquois, as we were told? She would certainly have returned home if she had not been eaten. I shall never cease to feel her loss, for she was a charming woman; and our brother undoubtedly had wit enough to have made a handsome fortune.'

They were still indulging these tender memories when they saw a little boat entering the bay of Rance on the tide. It was from England and had brought some local produce for sale. The crew jumped ashore without taking any notice either of the Prior or of his sister, who was deeply shocked at such disrespect.

Very different was the behaviour of a fine young man who leapt over the heads of his companions and landed face to face with the lady. He gave her a nod, as he was not accustomed to bowing. His face and his apparel attracted the attention of the brother and sister. He was bareheaded and barelegged, with only sandals on his feet, while his head was adorned with long hair in plaits. A short doublet added grace to a figure which was at once martial and gentle in bearing. In one hand he carried a small bottle of Barbados water, and in the other a kind of purse in which were a goblet and some first-rate ship's biscuits. He addressed Mademoiselle de Kerkabon and her brother in excellent French, and offered them some of the Barbados water, which he drank with them. He then gave them some more, and his behaviour throughout was so easy and natural that the brother and sister were charmed with it. They offered him their services and asked him who he was and where he was going. The young man replied that he himself did not know. He was full of curiosity, and wanted to see what the coast of France was like: that was why he had come, and he was then going back again.

The Prior guessed from his accent that he was not English, and took the liberty of asking from what country he came.

'I am a Huron,' replied the young man.

Mademoiselle de Kerkabon was surprised and delighted to find such a courteous Huron, and invited the young man to supper. There was no need to repeat the invitation, and they all three set off together for the Priory of Our Lady of the Mountain. The plump little woman could not take her eyes off him, and kept saying to her brother:

'Do look at that boy's complexion! It's all lilies and roses! What a lovely skin he has, for a Huron!'

'Yes indeed, sister,' replied the Prior.

She bombarded the traveller with questions, and the answers she received were always appropriate.

The news that there was a Huron at the Priory spread quickly. All the best society of the district made haste to have supper there. The Abbé de St Yves came with his pretty sister, a fine Low Breton girl who had been very well brought up. The Magistrate and the tax collector and their wives were there too. The stranger was given a seat between Mademoiselle de Kerkabon and Mademoiselle de St Yves. He was the centre of admiration and the target for a continual barrage of questions and conversation; yet nothing disturbed the Huron, for his motto seemed to be that of Lord Bolingbroke, *Nil admirari*.

But in the end the noise was so great that he was tired out, and said to them politely but with a touch of firmness: 'Gentlemen, in my country we speak one at a time; how can I answer you when you prevent me from hearing what you say?'

Reason always brings people to their senses for a short time. Silence fell. It was broken by the Magistrate, never one to miss an opportunity for monopolizing a stranger in anyone's house, and famous throughout the province for his inquisitiveness. Opening his mouth some six inches, he began:

'Sir, what are you called?'

'I have always been known as "The Child of Nature",' replied the Huron, 'and in England they gave me that name too, because I always say straight out what I think, just as I always do what I like.'

'You were born a Huron, Sir, but how is it that you managed to get to England?'

'It was because I was taken there. I was captured by the English after a fight in which I defended myself pretty well. The English admire courage because they are courageous themselves, and as they are also as honourable as we are, they gave me the choice of being sent back to my relatives or coming to England. I chose the latter, because I am by nature a keen traveller.'

'But, Sir,' protested the Magistrate, in his pompous voice, 'how could you bring yourself to leave your father and mother as you did?'

'I never knew either my father or my mother,' replied the stranger.

'Never knew his father or his mother!' echoed each member of the party, in tones of pity.

'We will take their place,' declared the lady of the house to her brother, the Prior. 'How attractive this Huron is!'

The Child of Nature thanked her warmly in his noble and dignified manner, and gave her to understand that he lacked for nothing.

'It seems to me, Monsieur Huron,' said the grave Magistrate, 'that you speak remarkably good French for one of your nationality.'

'That is because I learnt it from a Frenchman,' came the reply. 'One whom we took prisoner in Huronia when I was quite young, and to whom I became much attached. Anything I wish to learn, I can always master quickly. Moreover, when I arrived at Plymouth, I found there one of your French refugees whom for some reason you call Huguenots. He helped me to make further progress in the knowledge of your language, and as soon as I could make myself understood I came to see your country, because I am fond of the French, when they do not ask too many questions.'

Disregarding this hint, the Abbé de St Yves asked him which of the three languages he liked best, Huron, English, or French.

'Huron, of course,' replied the Child of Nature.

'Can it really be possible?' exclaimed Mademoiselle de Kerkabon. 'I had always believed that French was the most beautiful of all languages, except Low Breton.'

Then they all started asking about Huron. What was the word for tobacco in that language?

'*Taya*,' he replied.

And how does one say 'to eat'?

'*Essenten*,' he answered.

Mademoiselle de Kerkabon insisted on knowing the phrase for 'making love'; he said it was *trovander*, and maintained, quite reasonably, that these words were just as good as their French and English equivalents. The guests were all delighted with *trovander*.

The Prior left the table for a moment to consult the Huron grammar in his library, which had been given him by the Reverend Father Sagan Théodat, a famous Franciscan missionary. He returned in transports of tenderness and joy, for he now recognized the Child of Nature as a true Huron. The discussion turned for a time to the multiplicity of tongues, and it was agreed that all the world would certainly have spoken French, if it had not been for the incident of the Tower of Babel.

The inquisitive Magistrate had somewhat mistrusted this new character; now however he began to feel greater respect for him, and he spoke more politely than hitherto. But his pains were lost upon the Child of Nature.

Mademoiselle de St Yves was very curious to know how people made love in the land of the Hurons.

'They do fine deeds so as to give pleasure to people who look like you,' he replied.

This remark was received with applause and astonishment. Mademoiselle de St Yves blushed with delight. Mademoiselle de Kerkabon also blushed, but with less delight – she felt that the gallantry should have been addressed to her. She was so kindhearted, however, that her affection for the Huron was in no way altered by this slight. With undiminished goodwill she next asked him how many mistresses he had had in Huronia.

'I had only one,' replied the Child of Nature. 'She was Mademoiselle Abacaba, the friend of my dear nurse. She was as straight as a sapling, as white as the ermine, as gentle as the lamb, as proud as the eagle, and as light-footed as the deer. One day when she was chasing a hare in our part of the country, about fifty leagues from our home, an ill-bred Algonquin, who lived a hundred leagues further on, came and took her hare from her. I heard about it, and running up club in hand I felled the Algonquin with a single blow, and laid him at the feet of my mistress, bound hand and foot. Abacaba's family wanted to eat him, but I never had a taste for that sort of feast, so I gave him his freedom and made a friend of him. Abacaba was so touched by my behaviour that she preferred me to all her other lovers. She would love me still, if a bear had not eaten her. I killed the bear, and for a long time wore its skin, but that gave me no great consolation.'

When Mademoiselle de St Yves heard this story she was secretly relieved to hear that the Child of Nature had had only one mistress and that Abacaba was dead, but she did not recognize the source of her pleasure. The eyes of the whole company were on the Child of Nature, and he was much praised for having prevented his companions from eating an Algonquin.

The relentless Magistrate could not contain his stream of questions, and eventually had to relieve his curiosity by asking to what religion the Huron belonged, and whether he had chosen the English form, the French, or the Huguenot.

'I follow my own religion,' said he, 'as you do yours.'

'Those wretched English!' exclaimed Mademoiselle de Kerkabon, wringing her hands. 'I see that they did not even think of getting him baptized.'

'Heavens above!' said Mademoiselle de St Yves. 'How has it come about that Hurons are not Catholics? Haven't the Reverend Jesuit Fathers converted them all yet?'

The Child of Nature assured her that in his country no one was converted. No true Huron had ever changed his opinions, and there was no such word as 'inconstancy' in the language. Mademoiselle de St Yves was delighted with this last remark.

'We'll baptize him, we'll baptize him,' said Mademoiselle de Kerkabon to the Prior. 'You shall have the honour, my dear brother, and I insist on being his godmother. The Abbé de St Yves shall stand godfather. It will be a brilliant ceremony, all Lower Brittany will be talking of it, and it will do us the greatest honour.'

The whole company supported the mistress of the house, and all the guests shouted: 'We'll baptize him.'

The Child of Nature's reply to this was that in England everyone was allowed to live as he liked. The proposal gave him no pleasure at all, and he maintained that Huron Law was worth at least as much as Low Breton Law. Finally he declared that he was leaving next day. They managed to finish his bottle of Barbados water, and then they all went to bed.

When the Child of Nature had been taken to his room, Mademoiselle de Kerkabon and her friend Mademoiselle de St Yves could not resist looking through the keyhole to see how a Huron slept. They noticed that he had spread the covers from his bed on the floor, and that he had settled down in the most graceful attitude in the world.

CHAPTER 2

*

THE CHILD OF NATURE IS RECOGNIZED
BY HIS RELATIVES

THE Child of Nature awoke as usual at daybreak with the crowing of the cock, 'the trumpet of day' as they call it in England and in Huronia. He was not like people in high-society who linger idly in their beds till the sun has run half his course, unable either to sleep or to get up, and who lose so many precious hours in that state halfway between life and death, yet are always complaining that life is too short.

He had covered five or six miles and finished off thirty head of game in as many shots, before coming back to find the Prior of Our Lady of the Mountain and his modest sister in their nightcaps taking a walk in their little garden. He laid at their feet all the game he had dispatched, and then begged them to accept, in recognition of their kind reception, a sort of little talisman which he always wore round his neck and which he now produced from under his shirt.

'It's the most precious thing I possess,' he told them. 'I have been assured that I should always be happy so long as I wear this little trinket, and now I give it you to secure your happiness.'

The Prior and the lady smiled tenderly at the Child of Nature's simplicity. The present consisted of two crudely painted miniatures held together by a greasy strap.

Mademoiselle de Kerkabon asked him whether they had painters in Huronia.

'No,' replied the Child of Nature. 'This rarity came to me from my nurse. All that I know of it is that her husband acquired it as spoils of war from some French Canadians.'

The Prior looked closely at the portraits. His colour changed, and he became so agitated that his hands trembled.

'By Our Lady of the Mountain,' he exclaimed. 'That's the face of my brother the Captain, I feel sure, and that's his wife's!'

Mademoiselle de Kerkabon examined them with the same excitement, and came to the same conclusion. Both were rapt with astonishment. The joy they felt was mingled with grief, and tears of tenderness welled in their eyes. Their hearts throbbed, and they uttered cries as they snatched the portraits from each other, exchanging them at least twenty times a second.

They eagerly compared the portraits with the Huron's features, and implored him one after another, and both at the same time, to tell them when, where, and how these miniatures had fallen into the hands of his nurse. They agreed in their reckoning of the time that had elapsed since the Captain's departure; they remembered receiving news that he had reached the land of the Hurons, and that after that they had heard no more of him.

The Child of Nature had told them that he had known neither father nor mother. The Prior, who was an intelligent man, noticed that the Child of Nature had a small beard, and he knew very well that Hurons are beardless.

'His chin is downy, so he must be the son of a European. My brother and my sister-in-law never reappeared after the expedition against the Hurons in 1699. My nephew must still have been at the breast. His Huron nurse saved his life and was a mother to him.'

At last, after innumerable questions and answers, the Prior and his sister decided that the Huron really was their own nephew. They embraced him with tears in their eyes, and the young man laughed at the idea of a Huron being the nephew of a Breton Prior.

At this point the other guests appeared. Monsieur de St Yves, who was a great physiognomist, compared both portraits with the Huron's face, and very cleverly pointed out that he had his mother's eyes, the late Captain Kerkabon's forehead and nose, and cheeks which belonged to both of them.

Mademoiselle de St Yves, who had never seen either the mother or the father, was in no doubt that the resemblance was perfect. They were astonished at the ways of Providence, and at the chain of events in this world. At last, such was their persuasion, nay conviction, about his birth, that the Child of Nature himself consented to be the nephew of the Prior, saying that he would make as good an uncle as anyone else.

While thanks were given to God in the Church of Our Lady of the Mountain, the Huron, with an air of indifference, stayed in the house drinking until the English who had brought him came to tell him that they were ready to set sail and it was time to leave.

'Apparently,' said he, 'you have not been reunited with your uncles and aunts. I am staying here. Go back to Plymouth and you can have all my clothes, for I have no more need of anything as I am the nephew of a Prior.'

The English set sail, not caring overmuch whether the Huron had found relatives in Lower Brittany or not.

After uncle, aunt, and the whole company had sung the Te Deum, and the Magistrate had once more overwhelmed the Huron with questions, and they had exhausted everything that astonishment, joy, and tenderness could bring to mind, the Prior of the Mountain and the Abbé de St Yves decided that they must baptize the young man without further delay. But it was not the same thing christening a great Huron twenty-two years old as regenerating a baby who knows nothing of what is going on. He must be instructed, and that seemed to raise a difficulty, because the Abbé de St Yves did not imagine that a man not born in France could have any common sense.

The Prior, on the other hand, reminded the company that

although his nephew had not had the good fortune to be born in Lower Brittany, he had intelligence none the less, as they could judge from his replies; and surely he had been greatly blessed by nature in both his parents.

The first question was, had he read any books? He said he had read an English translation of Rabelais, and some extracts from Shakespeare, which he knew by heart; these were books which he had found in the cabin of the vessel which brought him from America to Plymouth, and they had given him great pleasure. The Magistrate seized the opportunity to question him about these books.

'I admit,' said the Huron, 'that I thought I understood something, and didn't fathom the rest.'

The Abbé de St Yves reflected that this had always been his own way of reading, and that of most other people.

'You have read the Bible, of course?' he asked the Huron.

'Never, Monsieur l'Abbé,' was the reply. 'It was not among the Captain's books. I have never heard of it.'

'Just like those accursed English!' cried Mademoiselle de Kerkabon. 'A play by Shakespeare, a plum pudding, a bottle of rum, mean more to them than the Pentateuch! And so, they have never converted anybody in America. There's no doubt about it, they are cursed by God; we shall take Jamaica and Virginia from them in no time!'

Be that as it may, the most skilful tailor in St Malo was sent for to clothe the Child of Nature from head to foot. The party broke up; the Magistrate went off to ask his questions elsewhere. Mademoiselle de St Yves could not tear herself away and kept turning round to look at the Child of Nature, who bowed to her more deeply than he had ever done to anyone in his life.

Before the Magistrate said farewell, he introduced Mademoiselle de St Yves to his great booby of a son just fresh from school; but she hardly noticed him, so preoccupied was she with the politeness of the Huron.

CHAPTER 3

*

THE CONVERSION OF THE CHILD OF NATURE

IT occurred to the Prior that as he was getting on in years and God had sent him a nephew for his consolation, he might be able to hand his living over to him, if only he could get him baptized and into Holy Orders.

The Child of Nature had an excellent memory. The vigour of his Breton constitution, fortified by the climate of Canada, had made his head so strong that he hardly felt a knock on the outside, while an impression on the inside was there for ever; he had never forgotten anything. As he had not had his head stuffed in childhood with the trivialities and stupidities which overburden ours, his understanding was lively and fresh, and everything he learned entered an unclouded brain. At last the Prior decided to make him read the New Testament.

The Child of Nature devoured it with much pleasure; but not knowing where or when all the events reported in the Book took place, he naturally assumed that the setting was Lower Brittany; he swore that he would cut off Caiaphas's nose and ears, and Pilate's too, if he ever came across the scoundrels.

His uncle was delighted to find him so well disposed, and soon put him right. He praised his enthusiasm, but pointed out how useless it was, since the fellows had died about sixteen hundred and ninety years ago. The Child of Nature soon knew nearly all the Book by heart. Every now and then he produced difficulties which gave the Prior a good deal of trouble. He was often obliged to consult the Abbé de St Yves, who had no answer either and had to summon a Low-Breton Jesuit to complete the Huron's conversion.

Grace at last prevailed, and the Child of Nature promised to become a Christian.

He had no doubt that the first step was to be circumcised, for as he said, 'There's not a single person in the Book I have been given to read who had not been; there is no doubt I must sacrifice my foreskin, and the sooner the better!' He wasted no time in deliberation, but sent at once for the village surgeon and begged him to perform the operation, rejoicing in the infinite pleasure it would give to Mademoiselle de Kerkabon and to all the company once it had been done. The village sawbones, who had never performed this operation, thought it best to warn the family, who uttered cries of distress. The good Mademoiselle de Kerkabon was terrified lest her nephew, who seemed so resolute and impetuous, should attempt the operation himself and bungle it, and that sad effects might result which are always a matter of concern to the ladies, such is the kindness of their hearts.

The Prior put the Huron's ideas in order once more, and made it clear that circumcision was no longer fashionable; baptism, he said, was much gentler and healthier, and the law of grace was not the same as the law of rigour. The Child of Nature argued, but his honesty and commonsense enabled him to acknowledge his mistake, which happens very rarely in Europe when people argue; at last he promised to be baptized whenever they liked.

The essential preliminary was confession, and this proved the greatest obstacle. In his pocket he always carried the Book his uncle had given him, and being unable to find that a single apostle had ever gone to confession, he became very obstinate. The Prior silenced him by showing him the passage in the Epistle of St James which has been such a stumbling block to heretics: *'Confess your sins one to another'*. The Huron gave way, and confessed to a monk. When he had finished, he pulled the monk out of the confessional, seized him with his powerful arm, made him change places, and forced him to his knees in front of him.

'Now, my friend,' said he, '*confess your sins one to another.*
I've told you my sins. You shan't leave this place until you
have told me yours.'

As he spoke, he leant his great knee against the chest of the
opposing party. The monk howled and screamed until the
church resounded. At the noise, people ran up and saw the
would-be communicant pommelling the monk in the name
of St James the Less. The joy of baptizing an English and
Huron Low-Breton was so great that this singular behaviour
was overlooked. And many theologians who were consulted
thought that confession was not strictly necessary, since
baptism took the place of everything.

A day was fixed with the Bishop of St Malo; understand-
ably flattered at the prospect of baptizing a Huron, he arrived
in a splendid equipage attended by his clergy. Mademoiselle
de St Yves praised God as she put on her most handsome dress
and sent for a hairdresser from St Malo in order to shine at
the ceremony. The inquisitive Magistrate turned up, with all
the countryside. The church was magnificently decorated. But
when the time came to lead the Huron to the baptismal font,
he was not to be found.

His uncle and aunt searched everywhere for him. They
thought he had gone hunting as usual, and all the guests
helped to search the woods and neighbouring villages, but
there was no news of the Huron.

They began to fear that he might have gone back to
England, for they remembered hearing him mention how
much he liked that country. The Prior and his sister were
convinced that there was no baptism over there, and trembled
for the soul of their nephew. The Bishop was dumbfounded,
and made ready to return; the Prior and the Abbé de St Yves
were in despair, and the Magistrate questioned all the passers-
by with his usual pomposity. Mademoiselle de Kerkabon
wept. Not so Mademoiselle de St Yves; but she sighed deeply
in a way which suggested a great liking for the sacraments.
The two women were wandering sadly among the willows

and reeds which border the little river Rance when they saw in mid-stream a tall pale figure, with its hands crossed on its breast. They shrieked and turned away; but curiosity triumphing over every other consideration, they soon crept quietly back among the reeds until they were sure of not being observed, for they wished to see what it was all about.

CHAPTER 4

*

THE CHILD OF NATURE BAPTIZED

THE Prior and the Abbé hurried to the scene and asked the Child of Nature what he was doing there.

'Why, what do you imagine? I am waiting for my baptism! I have been in the water up to my neck for a whole hour, and it's not fair to let me freeze to death.'

'My dear nephew,' said the Prior, tenderly, 'this is not the way we baptize people in Lower Brittany. Put on your clothes again, and come with us.'

Mademoiselle de St Yves heard this conversation, and whispered to her companion: 'Do you think he will put his clothes on straight away?'

Meanwhile the Huron was arguing with the Prior: 'You won't take me in so easily this time as you did before! I have been studying hard since then, and I am quite certain that this is the only way to be baptized. Queen Candace's eunuch was baptized in a stream, and I defy you to show me a single case in the Book you have given me where it was done differently! I will be baptized in the river, or not at all!'

It was in vain to try to persuade him that customs had changed, because as a Huron and a Breton he was naturally stubborn, and kept coming back to Queen Candace's eunuch. And although his aunt and Mademoiselle de St Yves, having watched him from among the willows, might well have told him that it was not for him to follow such an example, they were silenced by their admirable discretion. The Bishop himself was gracious enough to come and talk to him, but it was of no avail, for the Huron argued with the Bishop.

'Show me,' he asked him, 'one single instance, in the Book

my uncle gave me, of a man who was not baptized in a river, and I will do all you want.'

In despair, his aunt remembered the marked preference her nephew had shown for Mademoiselle de St Yves: on the first occasion that he had made a bow, he had bowed more deeply to her than to anyone else present, and not even the Bishop had been greeted with the respect and cordiality he had shown to that beautiful young lady. She made up her mind to appeal to her in this embarrassing situation, and begged her to use her favoured position to persuade the Huron to let himself be baptized in the same manner as the Bretons, for she did not believe that her nephew could ever be a Christian if he persisted in wanting to be baptized in running water.

Mademoiselle de St Yves, blushing with secret pleasure at being given such an important commission, approached him modestly and clasped his hand with a noble gesture:

'Won't you do something for me?' she said. And as she spoke the words she lowered her eyes and raised them, with a most moving grace.

'Oh, Madam! I will do anything you wish, anything you command; baptism by water, baptism by fire, baptism by blood, there is nothing I would refuse you.'

Mademoiselle de St Yves won the glory of accomplishing with two words what neither the persuasions of the Prior, nor the repeated interrogations of the Magistrate, nor even the reasonings of the Bishop, had been able to achieve. She enjoyed her triumph, but she did not yet realize the extent of it.

The baptism was both administered and received with full decorum; great was the magnificence, and universal the pleasure. The uncle and aunt relinquished to the Abbé de St Yves and his sister the honour of standing as godparents. Mademoiselle de St Yves was radiant with joy at finding herself a godmother. She did not know to what bondage this great title subjected her, nor what would be the fatal consequences of accepting this honour.

As no ceremony has ever been complete without a great dinner, the company sat down to table after leaving the baptism. The scoffers of Lower Brittany remarked that at least it was not necessary to baptize the wine. The Prior remarked that wine, according to Solomon, rejoices the heart of man. The Bishop added that the patriarch Judah was to tie his young ass to the vine and steep his cloak in the blood of the grape. He himself regretted that this was impossible in Lower Brittany, where the Lord had not provided vines. Each guest tried to be witty about the Huron's baptism, and to address compliments to the godmother. The ever-curious Magistrate asked the Huron if he would be faithful to his vows.

'How can you imagine I should be false to my promises,' replied the Huron, 'when I made them in the presence of Mademoiselle de St Yves?'

The Huron grew excited, and drank his godmother's health many times over.

'If I had been baptized at your hands,' he cried, 'I believe that the cold water would have burnt me as it was poured over the back of my neck.'

The Magistrate thought this speech too poetic, for he did not know how familiarly allegory is used in Canada. But it pleased the godmother immensely.

The name of Hercules had been given to the newly baptized Christian. The Bishop of St Malo kept asking who this saint could be, for he had never heard him mentioned. The Jesuit, who was very learned, was able to tell him that he was a saint who had performed twelve miracles. There was indeed a thirteenth, worth all the others, but which it did not become a Jesuit to describe – the feat of transforming fifty maidens into women in a single night. A wag who was present warmly praised this miracle. All the ladies lowered their eyes, and judged from the Huron's features that he was a worthy successor to the saint whose name he bore.

CHAPTER 5

*

THE CHILD OF NATURE IN LOVE

IT must be admitted that from the time of this baptism and
dinner Mademoiselle de St Yves felt a passionate longing for
the Bishop to make her a participant in some other beautiful
sacrament with Monsieur Hercules, the Child of Nature. She
was too well brought up and too modest, however, to give
these tender sentiments full rein even to herself; but if a look,
a word, a gesture, or a thought escaped her, she concealed it
in a veil of modesty that was infinitely charming. She was
tender and lively, and she was wise.

As soon as the Bishop had departed, the Child of Nature
and Mademoiselle de St Yves found themselves together without noticing that the one had sought the other's company.
They talked to each other without having thought what they
would say. The Child of Nature told her immediately that he
loved her with all his heart, and that the beautiful Abacaba,
whom he had worshipped in his own country, was not to be
compared to her. The lady replied, with her usual modesty,
that he must speak straight away to his uncle the Prior, and
to his aunt; she for her part would drop a word into her
dear brother's ear, and she was confident that they would
all give their consent.

The Huron replied that there was no need for anyone's
consent, and that he thought it was quite ridiculous to go
and ask others what to do; for when two parties were agreed,
there was no need of a third to bring them together.

'I don't consult anyone,' he said, 'when I want to have
breakfast, or to go hunting, or to go to sleep, though I quite
understand that in love it's not a bad idea to have the consent
of the person concerned. But as I am not in love with my

uncle or my aunt, I have no need to consult them over this; and if you take my advice, you'll leave the Abbé de St Yves out of it as well.'

Of course the lovely Breton used all her tact to reduce her Huron to a state of decorum. She even became angry, but she soon relented. There is no knowing how the conversation would have ended if the Abbé had not appeared at sunset to take his sister home. The Child of Nature let his uncle and aunt retire to bed, for they were a little tired after the ceremony and their lengthy dinner. He spent part of the night composing verses to his beloved in the Huron language, for one must remember that love will make lovers into poets the whole world over.

Next morning his uncle spoke to him after breakfast, in the presence of Mademoiselle de Kerkabon, who was much moved by the scene:

'Heaven be praised, my dear nephew, that you have the honour of being a Christian and a Low Breton! But this is not enough. I am getting on in years. My brother left only a small plot of ground worth very little; but I have a fine Priory. If you will only be ordained a sub-deacon, as I hope you will, I will resign my Priory to you, and you will live very comfortably, after being the consolation of my old age.'

'Much good may it do you, my dear uncle,' replied the Child of Nature. 'You must live as long as you can. I have no idea what it means to be a sub-deacon, nor to resign; but anything will suit me so long as I can have Mademoiselle de St Yves.'

'Good Heavens, nephew, what are you talking about? Are you really so much in love with that beautiful girl?'

'Yes, uncle, indeed I am.'

'I am sorry, nephew, but it is quite impossible for you to marry her.'

'On the contrary, uncle, it's altogether possible. She not only took my hand when she left me, but she promised to be my wife, and I shall certainly marry her.'

'I tell you it is out of the question. She is your godmother. It is a deadly sin for a godmother to take her godson's hand! A man is forbidden to marry his godmother; the laws of Heaven and earth are against it.'

'I believe you must be teasing me, uncle! Why should it be forbidden to marry one's godmother when she is young and pretty? I saw nothing in the Book you gave me to say that it was wrong to marry girls who have helped people to be baptized. I notice every day that innumerable things go on here which are not in your Book, and that nobody follows what it says. I own it surprises me, it shocks me. If I am deprived of the lovely St Yves under pretext of my baptism, I warn you I shall carry her off and unbaptize myself.'

The Prior was confounded; and his sister burst into tears.

'My dear brother,' said she, 'our nephew mustn't damn himself. Surely our Holy Father the Pope can give him a dispensation, and then he will be able to live a happy Christian life with his beloved.'

The Child of Nature embraced his aunt.

'Tell me, who is this delightful man,' he asked, 'who is so kind to boys and girls in love? I'll go and speak to him straight away.'

They explained to him who the Pope was, and the Child of Nature was even more astonished than before.

'There is not a word of all this in your Book, my dear uncle. I have travelled; I know what the sea is like. Here we are on the shores of the Atlantic. It's a ridiculous idea, quite incomprehensible, that I should leave Mademoiselle de St Yves to go and ask permission to love her from a man who lives by the Mediterranean, four hundred leagues from here. Besides, I shouldn't understand what he said! I am going straight to the Abbé de St Yves, who lives only a league from here, and I tell you I shall marry my darling this day.'

While he was still talking, the Magistrate entered, and as usual wanted to know where he was going.

'I am going to be married,' replied the Child of Nature, as

he ran off; and a quarter of an hour later he was already at the house of his charming and beloved Breton, who was still asleep.

Meanwhile Mademoiselle de Kerkabon was remarking to the Prior with a sigh, 'Brother, you'll never make our nephew a sub-deacon.'

The Magistrate was very much displeased by this expedition, because he intended his son to marry Mademoiselle de St Yves; and this son was even more stupid and unbearable than his father.

CHAPTER 6

*

THE CHILD OF NATURE RUSHES TO HIS
MISTRESS AND BECOMES ENRAGED

THE Child of Nature had no sooner arrived than he asked an old servant the way to her mistress's room. He gave a hearty push at the door, which was not securely fastened, and flew towards the bed. Mademoiselle de St Yves woke up with a start, and cried out:

'Good Heavens! You here! Can it be you? Stop it at once, what do you think you are doing?'

He replied, 'I am going to marry you,' and indeed he would have made her his, if she had not fought him off with all the decency of a girl who has been well brought up.

The Child of Nature had no intention of being trifled with; he regarded all such affectations as utterly silly.

'This is not how my first mistress, Mademoiselle Abacaba, behaved! You have no honesty; you give me your word that you'll marry me, and now you go back on it. This is breaking the first rules of honourable behaviour. I'll teach you to keep your word, and set you on the path of virtue.'

The Child of Nature's own virtue was virile and fearless, worthy of his patron saint Hercules, whose name he had been given at his baptism, and he was about to give it full scope. But the lady's virtue was of a more discreet nature; and her piercing cries summoned the good Abbé de St Yves and his housekeeper, as well as a devout old servant and a parish priest. The sight of these people diminished the assailant's ardour.

'Heavens above, my dear neighbour,' said the Abbé, 'what do you think you are doing?'

'My duty,' replied the young man. 'I am keeping my vows, and they are sacred.'

Mademoiselle de St Yves blushed as she covered herself up, while the Child of Nature was taken into another room. The Abbé pointed out to him the enormity of his proceedings, and he defended himself by citing the laws of nature, with which he was perfectly well acquainted. The Abbé maintained that positive law should always take precedence, and that, without the conventions men have accepted, the law of nature would almost always result in natural brigandage.

'We have to have lawyers, priests, witnesses, contracts, and dispensations,' said he. In reply the Child of Nature made the observation that savages have always made:

'Then you must be very dishonest, if you need so many precautions amongst you.'

The Abbé had some trouble in resolving this difficulty.

'I admit,' he said, 'that there are many rogues and cheats among us; and there would be just as many among the Hurons if they were all collected together in a large town. But we also have some wise, honest, and enlightened spirits, and it is these men who have made the laws. The more virtuous the man, the more he should submit to them; thus we set an example to profligates, who respect a curb that virtue voluntarily imposes.'

The Child of Nature was impressed by this reply. We have already noticed that he was a sensible fellow. He was calmed by flattering words, and given hopes for the future, two traps by which men are caught on both sides of the world. He was even allowed to see Mademoiselle de St Yves, once she had finished dressing. All this took place with the utmost decorum; at the same time, however, the sparkling eyes of Hercules kept his mistress blushing and the company all in a tremble.

There was great difficulty in persuading him to return to his family. Once more the power of the lovely St Yves had to be used; the more she felt her influence over him, the more she loved him. She persuaded him to go, and she was sorry to have done so. When at last he had gone, the Abbé, who was Mademoiselle de St Yves's guardian as well as her elder brother by many years, made up his mind to screen his pupil from the eagerness of this terrible lover. He went off to consult the Magistrate, who advised him to confine the poor girl in a convent, as he still had hopes of the Abbé's sister for his son. It was a terrible blow. One could expect bitter protests over being put into a convent even from someone with untroubled feelings; but for a girl in love, and for one so good and tender too, it was enough to drive her to despair.

Meanwhile the Child of Nature was back at the Prior's and was telling the whole story with his usual naïveté. He met with the same remonstrances, which had some effect on his mind, but none at all on his feelings. Next day he was proposing to go back to his darling and reason with her about the laws of nature and the laws of convention, but he was prevented by the Magistrate, who informed him with ill-concealed delight that she was in a convent.

'All right,' said he, 'I will go and reason with her in the convent.'

'You cannot do that,' said the Magistrate, and explained to him at great length what a convent is, and its derivation from the Latin *conventus*, meaning an assembly. But the Huron could not understand why he could not be admitted to the assembly. He became really furious, however, when he eventually grasped that this assembly was a kind of prison for keeping girls locked up, a horrible idea, unheard-of among the Hurons and the English. He felt like his patron Hercules when Eurytus king of Oechalia, who was no less cruel than the Abbé de St Yves, refused him his lovely daughter Iole, who was no less lovely than the Abbé's sister. He had a mind to go and set fire to the convent, and carry off his mistress or be burnt with her, proposals that terrified

Mademoiselle de Kerkabon, who gave up all hopes of seeing her nephew a sub-deacon, and murmured through her tears that he seemed to be possessed of the devil ever since he was baptized.

CHAPTER 7

*

THE CHILD OF NATURE REPELS THE ENGLISH

PLUNGED in deepest melancholy, the Child of Nature directed his steps towards the seashore. His double-barrelled gun was at his shoulder, his great cutlass at his side. Every now and then he shot a few birds, and was often tempted to shoot himself, but the thought of Mademoiselle de St Yves still made life worth living. Sometimes he cursed his uncle, his aunt, the whole of Lower Brittany, and his baptism; but sometimes he blessed them, because through them he had come to know his beloved. He made up his mind to go and burn down the convent, and then stopped short for fear of burning his mistress. The waves of the Channel are not more buffeted by the east and west winds than his heart was by so many contrary impulses.

He was striding along without knowing where he was going, when he heard the sound of a drum. In the distance he saw a crowd of people, half of them running towards the shore, the other half running away. Shouts rent the air on all sides. Courage and curiosity drove him at full speed towards the source of all the clamour, and he reached it in four bounds. He was immediately recognized by the Commandant of the Militia, who had met him at supper with the Prior.

'Ah, it's the Child of Nature,' cried the commandant. 'He will fight for us,' and the troops, who had been petrified with fear, rallied at his words and shouted:

'It's the Child of Nature, the Child of Nature.'

'Pray tell me, gentlemen,' said he, 'what is it all about. Why are you so dismayed? Have your mistresses all been shut up in convents?'

At this, a hundred excited voices cried out: 'Don't you see that the English are landing?'

'What of it?' replied the Huron. 'They are fine folk, the English. They have never tried to make me a sub-deacon or carried off my mistress.'

The commandant explained to him that the English had come to pillage the Abbey of the Mountain, drink his uncle's wine, and perhaps carry off Mademoiselle de St Yves. The little vessel from which he had landed in Brittany had only come to reconnoitre the coast; this was an act of aggression committed without declaring war on the King of France, and the province was in danger.

'Oh, if that's the case, they are violating the law of nature. But leave it to me. I have spent a long time among them, and understand their language. Let me talk to them, for I cannot believe that they have such a wicked plan.'

During this conversation, the English squadron drew near. The Huron ran towards them, jumped into a little boat, reached the Admiral's vessel, and climbed on board. He then asked whether it was true that they had come to ravage the country without declaring war in an honest manner. The Admiral and all on board burst into a hearty laugh; they gave him a drink of punch, and sent him back again.

The Child of Nature was deeply offended. He now had no other thought than that of putting up a good fight against his former friends, for the sake of his compatriots and his uncle the Prior. The gentry from all around came running up, and he joined them. They had a few cannon, which he loaded, aimed, and fired one after the other. As the English disembarked, he rushed at them and killed three with his own hand; he even wounded the Admiral who had laughed at him. His courage was an inspiration to the whole militia; the English were forced back to their ships, and the shores resounded with cries of victory:

'Long live the King. Long live the Child of Nature.'

They all embraced him, and hurried to staunch the blood from a few scratches he had received.

'If only Mademoiselle de St Yves were here,' he sighed, 'she would bandage me.'

The Magistrate, who had been hiding in his cellar while the battle lasted, came to congratulate him like the others. But he was not a little surprised when he heard Monsieur Hercules remarking to a handful of willing young men who surrounded him: 'Saving the Abbey of the Mountain is nothing, lads; there's a girl to be rescued!'

This was enough to rouse every one of these ardent youngsters. They were already flocking after him, making straight for the convent, and if the Magistrate had not immediately warned the commanding officer, and the merry band had not been pursued, it would have been all over. The Child of Nature was brought back to his uncle and aunt, who received him with tears of joy.

'I can quite see that you will never be a sub-deacon, or a prior,' his uncle told him. 'You will be an even braver officer than my brother the captain, and I daresay you'll be just as poor.'

Mademoiselle de Kerkabon wept over him as she embraced him and said: 'He will be killed as my brother was. It would be much better for him to be a sub-deacon.'

In the course of the battle the Child of Nature had picked up a large purse full of guineas, which had probably been dropped by the Admiral. He had no doubt that with all this money he could buy up the whole of Lower Brittany and, more particularly, make Mademoiselle de St Yves a great lady. But what he was advised to do was to make a journey to Versailles to receive the reward for his services. The mayor and the chief officers loaded him with testimonials. His aunt and uncle gave their approval to their nephew's journey, and saw no difficulty about his gaining access to the King. This alone would give him immense prestige in the province; and in so good a cause these kindly people added to his English purse a considerable sum from their savings. The Child of Nature said to himself:

'When I see the King, I'll ask him for the hand of Mademoiselle de St Yves in marriage, and surely he will not refuse me.'

So he set off amid the applause of the whole canton, overwhelmed with embraces, drenched with his aunt's tears, blessed by his uncle, and recommending his spirit to the lovely St Yves.

*

THE CHILD OF NATURE GOES TO COURT
AND ON THE WAY HAS SUPPER
WITH SOME HUGUENOTS

THE Child of Nature took the coach to Saumur, for at that time there was no other means of travel. When he arrived, he was surprised to find the place almost deserted, and to see many families moving out. He was told that six years earlier the population of Saumur had been over fifteen thousand, but that at present it was less than six thousand. This was the topic of discussion over supper at his inn. There were several Protestants at table, some complaining bitterly and some trembling with anger, while others wept as they lamented:

'*Nos dulcia linquimus arva, nos patriam fugimus.*'

The Child of Nature, who knew no Latin, was told that these words meant: 'We are leaving the country we love, we are fleeing from the land where we were born.'

'And why are you leaving your country, gentlemen?'

'Because they want us to recognize the Pope.'

'And why shouldn't you recognize him? You haven't any godmothers you want to marry, have you? Because I was told that it was he that would give me permission.'

'Oh, but this Pope, Sir, he says he rules over kings' dominions!'

'But, gentlemen, what is your profession?'

'Most of us are drapers and manufacturers, Sir.'

'Well, if your Pope says he is going to rule over your cloths and your factories, you are quite right not to recognize him. But as for kings, that's their business. Why meddle in it?'

At this point a little man in black began to speak, and

135

enlarged in a very learned manner on the grievances of the company. He spoke with such energy of the Revocation of the Edict of Nantes, he waxed so pathetic over the fate of fifty thousand fugitive families, and another fifty thousand who had been converted by quartering dragoons in their houses, that the Child of Nature found himself weeping in sympathy.

'But how is it,' he asked, 'that such a great king, whose fame has even reached the Hurons, should let himself be deprived of so many folk who would love him with their hearts and serve him with their hands?'

'It's because he has been deceived, like other great kings,' replied the man in black. 'He has been led to believe that he has only to say a word and everybody will think as he does, and that he could make us change our religion as quickly as his musician Lully can change the scenery in his operas. He has not only lost five or six thousand useful subjects already, but he has made enemies of them; and King William, who is the present ruler of England, has organized several regiments out of those very Frenchmen, who would otherwise have fought for their own king.

'This disaster is all the more surprising, because the reigning Pope, to whom Louis XIV has sacrificed part of his people, is his avowed enemy. After nine years, they still keep up a violent quarrel. It has gone so far that at last France is hoping to see the breaking of the yoke which has bound her for so many centuries to that foreigner, and more especially to give him no more money; which is the chief motive in the affairs of the world. It therefore looks as if this great monarch has been deceived about his interests as well as about the extent of his powers, and that his advisers have injured his reputation for magnanimity of heart.'

The Child of Nature became more and more moved by this account, and asked who the Frenchmen were who could thus deceive a monarch so dear to the Hurons?

'The Jesuits,' was the reply, 'and chiefly Father de La

Chaise, His Majesty's confessor. It is to be hoped that God will punish them one day, and that they will be driven out as now they drive us out. Is there any misfortune to equal ours? This fellow de Louvois attacks us with Jesuits and dragoons on all sides.'

'As for that, gentlemen,' replied the Child of Nature, who could no longer contain himself, 'I am on my way to Versailles to receive the reward for my services, and I will talk to this fellow de Louvois. I am told he is the man who directs campaigns from his office. I will see the King and I will let him know the truth. It is impossible not to acknowledge the truth of this once you see it. I will soon be back, to marry Mademoiselle de St Yves, and I invite you to the wedding.'

The good people began to think he must be a great nobleman travelling *incognito* by coach, while some of them took him for the King's jester.

Among those at table was a Jesuit in disguise, who acted as a spy for the Reverend Father de La Chaise. He took note of everything, and Father de La Chaise passed it on to Monseigneur de Louvois. The spy made his report, which arrived at Versailles almost at the same time as the Huron.

CHAPTER 9

THE ARRIVAL OF THE CHILD OF NATURE
AT VERSAILLES, AND HIS RECEPTION
AT COURT

THE Child of Nature alighted from his 'chamber-pot'* in the kitchen yard. He asked the chairmen what time the King could be seen. They laughed in his face, just as the English Admiral had done, and he treated them in just the same way; that is to say, he boxed their ears. They began to retaliate, and the scene would have been bloody had not a Breton gentleman who was one of the officers of the guard appeared and dispersed the rabble.

'You seem to me a brave man, sir,' said the traveller. 'I am the nephew of the Prior of Our Lady of the Mountain. I have killed some Englishmen, and I have come to speak to the King. I beg you to take me to his room.'

The officer was delighted to discover a gallant man from his own province who appeared ignorant of Court customs, and informed him that one did not go straight in and speak to the King, as it was necessary to be presented by Monseigneur de Louvois.

'Very well, take me to this Monseigneur de Louvois; no doubt he will conduct me to His Majesty.'

'To talk to Monseigneur de Louvois,' replied the officer, 'is even more difficult than to talk to His Majesty. But I will take you to Monsieur Alexandre, the First Secretary for War. It will be just as good as talking to the Minister.'

Off they went accordingly to see this Monsieur Alexandre,

* A coach plying between Paris and Versailles which looks like a little covered tipcart. [Voltaire's note.]

the First Secretary; but they could not be admitted. He was engaged with a lady of the Court, and had given orders that no one was to be allowed in.

'Never mind,' said the officer, 'that's no great loss. Let us go to Monsieur Alexandre's First Secretary. It will be just as good as talking to Monsieur Alexandre himself.'

The Huron followed him in astonishment, and they waited half an hour in a little antechamber.

'What's all this?' asked the Child of Nature. 'Is everyone invisible in this part of the world? It is much easier to fight the English in Lower Brittany than it is to find the people you have to deal with at Versailles.'

He passed the time by telling his compatriot about his love affairs. But the hour struck and recalled the officer to his post. They promised to meet again the next day, and the Child of Nature waited another half hour in the antechamber, dreaming of Mademoiselle de St Yves and the difficulty of speaking to Kings and First Secretaries.

At last the chief appeared.

'Sir,' said the Child of Nature, addressing him, 'if I had waited as long to repel the English as you have kept me waiting for audience, they would now be ravaging Lower Brittany at their leisure.'

These words attracted the Secretary's attention, and he said to the Breton: 'What do you want?'

'My reward,' replied the other. 'Here's proof of what I've done,' and he held out all his certificates. The Secretary read them, and told him that he would probably be allowed to buy himself a commission.

'What's that you say? I am to put down some money for driving the English off? To pay for the privilege of getting myself killed for you, while you sit here quietly giving audiences? You must be joking. I want a company of cavalry for nothing. I want the King to get Mademoiselle de St Yves out of her convent and give her to me in marriage. I want to plead with the King on behalf of fifty thousand families, whom I mean to restore to him. In short, I want to be useful, I want to be employed and get on in the world.'

'What is your name, Sir, that you talk so loudly?'

'Oh indeed,' replied the Child of Nature. 'So you haven't read my testimonials? That's the treatment you get, is it? My name is Hercules de Kerkabon, I have been baptized, I am lodging at the Blue Dial, and I shall complain of you to the King.'

The Secretary concluded, as the people of Saumur had done, that he was not quite right in the head, and did not take much notice of him.

The same day, the Reverend Father de La Chaise, confessor to Louis XIV, had received the letter from his spy accusing the Breton Kerkabon of taking sides with the Huguenots and condemning the conduct of the Jesuits. Monseigneur de Louvois, for his part, had received a letter from the inquisitive Magistrate describing the Huron as a young rogue who wanted to set fire to convents and carry off the girls.

The Child of Nature took a turn in the gardens of Versailles, which did not appeal to him, and dined like a Huron and a Low Breton; he went to bed with the delicious thought of seeing the King next day, obtaining the hand of Mademoiselle de St Yves in marriage, commanding at least a cavalry company, and ending the persecution of the Huguenots. He was indulging himself with these flattering visions when the police entered his room.

They first seized his double-barrelled gun and his great broadsword. Then they made a record of his ready money, and carried him off to that sinister fortress built by King Charles V, son of John II, near the rue St Antoine at the Tournelles gate.

I will leave you to imagine the astonishment of the Child of Nature on his way there. At first he thought it was a dream, and sat paralysed, until suddenly he was seized by a fit of anger which redoubled his strength. Grasping two of his guards by the throat, he threw them out of the carriage door and hurled himself after them, pulling along the third, who was trying to hold him back. The effort brought him to the ground, and he was tied up and put back in the carriage.

'Look at that!' he said. 'That's what one gets for chasing the English out of Lower Brittany. What would you say, my lovely St Yves, if you saw me in this state?'

At last they arrived at the quarters which were destined for him. He was borne in silence into the room where he was to be shut up, like a corpse that is carried to the cemetery. The room was already occupied by an old man, a 'hermit' from the Port Royal called Gordon, who had languished in it for two years.

'Hallo there,' said the chief of the myrmidons. 'Here's some company I've brought you.' Without more ado the huge bolts of the thick door were thrust into their sockets and secured with great bars. The two prisoners were cut off from the whole universe.

CHAPTER 10

THE CHILD OF NATURE IMPRISONED IN THE
BASTILLE WITH A JANSENIST

MONSIEUR GORDON was a lively and serene old man, who was experienced in two most important things, in making the best of adversity, and consoling the unfortunate. With a frank and compassionate expression he approached his companion, embraced him, and addressed him thus:

'Whoever you may be that come to share my tomb, you may be sure that I will always put aside my own troubles to soften yours in this infernal abyss to which we have been committed. Let us worship Providence, which has brought us here. Let us suffer in silence, and be hopeful.'

These words had the same effect on the youth as the English cordial which revives a dying man; it made him open his eyes a little with astonishment.

As soon as the first civilities had been exchanged, the gentleness of Gordon's conversation, and the interest which two unfortunates naturally take in one another, persuaded the Huron to open his heart and lay down the burden which was overwhelming him, though he was not pressed to do so. He could make no guess at the reason for his misfortune, which seemed to him an effect without a cause; and the worthy Gordon was as much astonished as he was.

'Surely the Lord must have great designs for you,' said the Jansenist to the Huron, 'since He has brought you all the way from Lake Ontario to England and then to France, has had you baptized in Lower Brittany, and then placed you here for your salvation!'

'Believe me,' replied the young man, 'it's the devil alone that has had a hand in my destiny, I'm thinking. My American compatriots would never have treated me with such barbarity. They have no notion of it. They are called "savages", and certainly they are uncouth; but they are decent folk, and the people of this country are refined blackguards. I must confess that I am much surprised to find I have come from the other side of the world to be shut up on this side behind four bolts with a priest. But I must not forget the prodigious number of men who leave one hemisphere to go and get themselves killed in the other, or who get shipwrecked on the way, and are food for fishes. I fail to see what gracious plans the Lord had for them either.'

Their dinner was handed to them through a grille. Conversation turned on Providence, on arbitrary arrest and imprisonment, and on the art of surviving the misfortunes to which every man is exposed in this world.

'I have been here for two years now,' said the old man, 'with nothing to console me but myself and some books, and I have never had a moment's ill humour.'

'But Monsieur Gordon,' exclaimed the Child of Nature, 'you are not in love with your godmother. If you knew Mademoiselle de St Yves, as I do, you would be in despair.'

As he uttered these words he could no longer refrain from weeping, and this made him feel a little better.

'How is it,' he wanted to know, 'that tears can bring relief? It seems to me they ought to have the opposite effect.'

'My son,' replied the good old man, 'everything inside us is purely physical. Each secretion is good for us, and everything that comforts the body comforts the soul. We are machines made by Providence.'

We have often had occasion to remark that the Child of Nature had a great deal of intelligence; he brooded upon this idea, which seemed to correspond to something within him. Eventually he asked his companion why his bodily machine had been for two years behind locks and bar.

'I am here by the efficacious grace of God,' replied Gordon. 'I am what is called a Jansenist; I knew Arnaud and Nicole.

We were persecuted by the Jesuits. We believe that the Pope is only a bishop like any other; and that is why Father de La Chaise obtained an order from the King, who is his penitent, to have me deprived of man's most precious possession, liberty, without so much as a trial.'

'That is very strange,' remarked the Child of Nature. 'The Pope seems to be at the bottom of all the troubles I have met so far. As for your efficacious grace, I must admit that I don't understand a word of it; but I think it was a great sign of grace that God has found me a man like you in the hour of my misery, a man who finds consolation for me which I thought I was incapable of receiving.'

Each day their conversation grew more interesting and more instructive, and the two captives grew warmly attached to each other. The old man was well-informed, and the young one was eager to learn. At the end of a month he was studying geometry, and he absorbed it fast. Gordon made him read Rohault's *Physics*, which was still fashionable, and he had the perspicacity to find nothing but uncertainties in it.

After that, he read the first volume of Malebranche's *Search for Truth*, a work which threw new light upon the subject for him.

'Can it be,' he exclaimed, 'that our imagination and our feelings deceive us to this extent? Our ideas are not based upon what we observe, and we have no means of forming them for ourselves!'

By the time he had read the second volume, he was less satisfied, and decided that it was easier to be destructive than constructive. His fellow-prisoner was astonished to find this uneducated young man coming to a conclusion of a much maturer mind, and formed a high opinion of his intelligence and a still deeper attachment to him.

'This Malebranche of yours,' the Child of Nature remarked one day, 'seems to me to have written half his book with the aid of his reason, and the other half under the influence of his imagination and his prejudices.'

A few days later, Gordon asked him what he thought about the soul, the way we receive ideas:

'What are your views on the passions, on divine grace, and on free will?'

'I have no opinions,' replied the Child of Nature. 'If I believe anything, it is that we are in the power of an eternal Being, just as the stars and the elements are. He controls us, and we are little cogs in the immense machine of which He is the soul. I believe, too, that He works by general laws and not with particular objects in view. That's as far as I can go; all the rest is an unfathomable depth of shadows.'

'But, my son, that would mean that the Lord was the author of evil!'

'But, Father, your theory of efficacious grace would also make God the author of evil, because it is certain that all would sin if this grace were denied them, and surely he that delivers us to evil must be the author of evil?'

The good old man was much distressed by this display of sincerity. He felt he was struggling in vain to extricate himself from the mire, and he poured out so many words which seemed to have sense yet meant nothing (like the chatter about physical predetermination) that the Child of Nature was moved to pity him. The question clearly depended on the origin of good and evil, and inevitably poor Gordon had to bring up in turn Pandora's box, the egg of Ormuzd which Ahriman pierced, the enmity between Typhon and Osiris, and finally original sin. The two ran hither and thither in this primeval darkness without ever meeting each other. But this romance of the soul succeeded in distracting attention from their misery; and by some sort of magic the thought of the calamities heaped upon the universe diminished their sense of their own afflictions; they did not dare to complain, when the whole world was suffering.

But when night came, the image of the lovely St Yves blotted out all these moral and metaphysical ideas from the mind of her lover. He woke up with tears in his eyes, and the old Jansenist forgot his efficacious grace, and the Abbé de St Cyran, and Jansen, in order to console a young man whom he believed to be in a state of mortal sin.

When they had finished discussing and disputing, they returned to their adventures, and after these useless reminiscences they took to reading, either separately or together. The young man's intelligence developed rapidly, especially in mathematics, and he would no doubt have gone a long way in this branch of study, had he not been so distracted by the thought of Mademoiselle de St Yves.

He read history and was saddened by it, for the world seemed to him altogether too wicked and miserable. After all, history is but a chronicle of crime and misery. The host of innocent and peaceloving people always disappears from view in this vast theatre, while the chief actors are nothing but evil and ambitious men. There seems to be no pleasure in History any more than in Tragedy, which languishes unless it is enlivened by passion, crime, and great misfortune. Clio as well as Melpomene must be armed with a dagger.

The history of France is as full of horrors as the rest. But there was so much to displease him in the early stages, so much that was dry in the middle period, so much that was petty even in the days of Henri IV – no sign of the great monuments and the bold discoveries which have done honour to other nations – that he was obliged to struggle with boredom in reading all the details of minor calamities confined to a corner of the world.

Gordon felt the same. They laughed with pity when the people concerned were the sovereigns of Fezensac, Fesansaguet, and Astarac, those tiny tracts in Armagnac, a subject for study which would interest only their descendants, if they had any.

The splendid centuries of the Roman republic made him indifferent for a time to the rest of the world, and his whole mind was engrossed in the spectacle of victorious Rome as lawgiver of the nations. He grew excited at the idea of a people who for seven hundred years were governed by enthusiasm for liberty and glory.

Thus the days passed, then weeks, then months, and he would have thought himself happy in this habitation of despair, if he had not been in love.

As a good-natured man he often felt sad as he remembered the worthy Prior of Our Lady of the Mountain and the affectionate Mademoiselle de Kerkabon. 'How ungrateful they will think I am,' he often said to himself, 'to get no news of me.'

This idea tormented him, and he was far more sorry for those he loved than he was for himself.

CHAPTER II

*

THE CHILD OF NATURE DEVELOPS
HIS TALENTS

READING enlarges the mind, and the company of an enlightened friend brings it comfort. Our captive was enjoying two benefits, neither of which he had tasted before.

'I shall be tempted to believe in metamorphoses,' he remarked, 'for I have been transformed from a brute into a man.'

He was allowed to spend some of his money, and amassed a choice collection of books. His friend encouraged him to set down his reflexions, and this is what he wrote on ancient history:

I imagine that the nations were for a long time in the state I have been in, that they were not educated until very late in life, and that for many centuries they lived only for the present moment, thinking little about the past and never about the future. I have travelled five or six hundred leagues across Canada, without discovering a single monument; nobody there knows anything about what his great-grandfather did. Would not that be the natural state of man? The human race on this continent seems to me superior to what is found over there. For several centuries they have cultivated themselves by the pursuit of art and learning. Is that because they have beards on their chins, and God has denied beards to the Americans? I do not believe it, because I see that the Chinese have scarcely any beard, and they have been cultivating the arts for more than five thousand years. For if they have records going back more than four thousand years, it stands to reason that they must have been united as a nation, and flourishing too for more than fifty centuries.

One thing in particular strikes me about this ancient history of China, and that is that nearly everything in it is credible and natural. I admire it because there are no prodigies in it, nothing out of the course of nature.

Why is it that all the other nations have given themselves fabulous origins? The ancient chroniclers of the history of France, who are not so very ancient, make out that the French are descended from one Francus, son of Hector. The Romans claimed that they were the issue of a Phrygian, though there is not a single word in their language that bears the least resemblance to the Phrygian tongue. The gods have lived for ten thousand years in Egypt, and the devils had inhabited Scythia, where they gave birth to the Huns. Before the time of Thucydides, I can find nothing but tales like that of Amadis and much less entertaining. They are concerned all the time with apparitions, oracles, prodigies, sorcery, metamorphoses, the interpretation of dreams: fantasies that control the destiny of the greatest empires and the smallest states. Here you find beasts that talk, there you find beasts that are worshipped, gods transformed into men and men into gods. If we must have fables, for heaven's sake let them at least be emblems of truth. I love philosophers' fables, but I laugh at children's, and I hate those that are foisted upon us by priests.

One day he came across a history of the emperor Justinian. He read there that some numskulls of Constantinople had put out an edict, in atrocious Greek, against the greatest captain of the century, because in the heat of conversation he had let fall these words:

'Truth shines with its own light, and you cannot illuminate the mind by flames from the stake.'

The numskulls declared that this statement was a heresy, or at any rate smelled of heresy, and that the contrary axiom was Catholic, universal, and Greek:

'You can only illuminate the mind by flames from the stake, and the truth cannot shine with its own light.'

This was the way these 'budge doctors' condemned many of the captain's sayings, and pronounced an edict against him.

'What on earth is this?' cried the Child of Nature. 'Such creatures as these pronouncing edicts!'

'These are not edicts,' sighed Gordon. 'These are counter-edicts, and were the laughing-stock of everyone in Constantinople, and first and foremost the Emperor. He was a wise prince and he knew how to manage numskulls in cap and gown so as to use them for the common good. He knew that these gentlemen and several other image-bearers had tried the patience of preceding emperors with their counter-edicts, on more important matters.'

'He did well,' replied the Child of Nature. 'Priests have to be both sustained and contained.'

He committed to paper many other observations which alarmed old Gordon.

'Can this be?' he said to himself. 'I have spent fifty years educating myself and I am afraid I shall never attain the natural commonsense of this half-savage boy! I fear I have been hard at work strengthening prejudices, whereas he listens only to the voice of nature.'

The worthy old fellow had some of those essays in criticism, those periodical pamphlets, in which writers who are themselves incapable of original work disparage the work of others, where creatures like Visé insult Racine, and where a Faidi can affront a Fénelon. The Child of Nature looked through some of them.

'They seem to me,' said he, 'to resemble those little flies which choose the finest horses and lay their eggs in their backsides; but that does not hinder the horses from running.' The two philosophers barely condescended to look at this excrement of literature.

They turned their attention next to studying the rudiments of astronomy. The Child of Nature sent for some globes, and was entranced by the magnificent spectacle.

'How hard it is,' he sighed, 'to scrape acquaintance with the sky only when I am deprived of the right to look at it! Jupiter and Saturn revolve in those immense spaces, millions of suns light up thousands of millions of worlds, and in this corner of the earth where my lot is cast there are people who deprive me, a seeing and thinking being, of all those worlds to which my sight could reach, and of this one where God decided I should be born! The light given to the whole universe is lost to me. It was not kept from me in those Northern latitudes where I passed my childhood and my youth. Without you, my dear Gordon, I should be utterly annihilated here.'

CHAPTER 12

*

THE CHILD OF NATURE'S OPINIONS ON PLAYS

THE Child of Nature was like one of those hardy trees which begin life in unpromising soil and throw out their roots and branches as soon as they are transplanted into a more favourable locality. Strange as it may seem, it was life in prison which provided this locality.

Among the books which occupied the leisure of the two captives, there was some poetry, some translations of Greek tragedy, and a few French plays. The love poetry he read filled the soul of our Child of Nature with both pleasure and grief, for it all spoke to him of his dear St Yves. La Fontaine's fable of the two pigeons touched him to the very heart, for it was so far beyond his power to return to his dovecot.

He was delighted with Molière, who made him acquainted with the customs of Paris and indeed of the human race.

'Which of his comedies is your favourite?'

'*Tartuffe*, without a doubt.'

'I agree with you,' said Gordon. 'It was a Tartuffe who plunged me into this dungeon, and perhaps it is the Tartuffes who are responsible for your misfortunes. What do you think of these Greek tragedies?'

'Good enough for the Greeks,' replied the Child of Nature.

But when he read our modern plays about Iphigenia, Phaedra, Andromache, and Athalia, he was in ecstasy; he sighed, he wept, and he learnt them by heart without even intending to.

'Read Corneille's *Rodogune*,' Gordon told him. 'They say that is the great masterpiece of the theatre. The other plays that have given you so much pleasure are not to be compared with it.'

Before he had finished the first page, the young man said to him: 'It isn't by the same author.'

'How do you know?'

'I can't tell yet. But these verses appeal neither to my ear nor to my heart.'

'Oh, that's only the versification,' replied Gordon.

The Child of Nature retorted: 'Why write in verse, then?'

He read the play with great care, and no other motive than to find pleasure in it; then he looked at his friend with dry and puzzled eyes, not knowing what to say. At last, pressed to describe what he had felt, he replied in these terms:

'I hardly understood the beginning, I was shocked by the middle, I was much moved by the last scene, although it seemed to me rather improbable. I could not feel concerned about any of the characters, and I have not remembered twenty lines, though I can remember them all when I like them.'

'But this play is considered to be the best we have.'

'If that is so,' replied the Huron, 'it is perhaps like so many people who do not deserve their positions. After all, it is a question of taste; no doubt mine isn't formed yet, and I could be mistaken. But, as you know, I am used to saying what I think, or rather what I feel. I suspect that men's judgements are often influenced by delusion, by fashion, or by caprice. I spoke straight from Nature, and my idea of Nature may be very imperfect, but it may also be that most people rarely consult Nature at all.'

Then he repeated some lines from Racine's *Iphigénie*, of which his head was full, and though he did not recite well, he put so much truth and earnestness into it that he reduced the old Jansenist to tears. After that, he read *Cinna*; it did not make him weep, but it impressed him.

CHAPTER 13

THE LOVELY ST YVES GOES TO VERSAILLES

THUS our unfortunate hero was finding more to enlighten
than to console him. His intelligence developed with powerful
and rapid strides, after having been so long starved; and as
nature completed her work in him, she took her revenge for
the outrages of fortune.

But what, meanwhile, had been happening to the Prior
and his worthy sister, and to the lovely St Yves in her en-
forced retreat? For the first month they were worried, and
by the third they were in distress, a prey to false conjectures
and ill-founded rumours. At the end of six months, they
thought he must be dead. At last Monsieur and Mademoiselle
Kerkabon learnt, from an old letter which one of the King's
Guard had sent home to Brittany, that a young man resem-
bling the Child of Nature had arrived one evening at Versailles, but had been carried off during the night, and that
no one had heard of him since.

'Our nephew must have done something stupid,' said
Mademoiselle de Kerkabon with a sigh. 'He will have got
himself into some awkward scrape! He's young, he's a Low
Breton, he could not know how to behave at Court. My dear
brother, I have never seen Versailles, or Paris either; here
is a good opportunity. Perhaps we shall find our poor nephew;
after all, he is our brother's son, and it is our duty to help
him. Who knows but we may eventually succeed in making
him a sub-deacon, when the fire of youth has cooled! He was
well disposed to learning. Do you remember how he used to
argue about the Old and the New Testament? We are
responsible for his soul, for it was we who had him baptized;
and Mademoiselle de St Yves whom he loves so dearly spends

her days weeping. Assuredly, we must go to Paris. If he is hidden in one of those vile bawdy-houses that I have heard so much about, we will rescue him.'

The Prior was moved by his sister's words; he went off to find the Bishop of St Malo, who had baptized the Huron, and asked for his protection and advice. The prelate approved of the journey, and gave the Prior letters of introduction, one of them addressed to Father de La Chaise, the King's confessor and the most important person in the kingdom, and others to Harlai, the Archbishop of Paris, and to Bossuet, the Bishop of Meaux.

The brother and sister set off at last; but when they reached Paris they found themselves as bewildered as if they were in a vast labyrinth, without a thread to guide them or any way out. Their means were modest, they needed carriages every day for reconnoitring, and they discovered nothing.

The Prior called upon the Reverend Father de La Chaise, but he had Mademoiselle du Tron with him, and could not give audience to Priors. He went to the Archbishop's door, but he was closeted with the lovely Madame de Lesdiguières on church business. He hurried to the country house of the Bishop of Meaux, but he was engaged with Mademoiselle de Mauléon in studying Madame Guyon's doctrine of mystic love. He did succeed, however, in getting a hearing from these two prelates, but they both declared that they could do nothing for his nephew, since he was not a sub-deacon.

At last he saw the Jesuit. The man received him with open arms, protesting that he had always had a particular regard for him, though in fact he had never known him. He swore that the Society of Jesus had always been attached to the Low Bretons.

'But your nephew,' he went on, 'has the misfortune to be a Huguenot, hasn't he?'

'Certainly not, Reverend Father.'

'There's nothing of the Jansenist about him?'

'I can assure Your Reverence that he is hardly even a Christian. It is only about eleven months since we baptized him.'

'That's good, that's good, we will look after him. Is your benefice of much value?'

'No, nothing much; and my nephew is very expensive.'

'Are there any Jansenists in the neighbourhood? Keep a sharp lookout for them, my dear Prior. They are more dangerous than Huguenots or atheists.'

'We have none at all, Reverend Father. We don't know what Jansenists are at Our Lady of the Mountain.'

'So much the better. That's splendid! There is nothing I wouldn't do for you.'

He took a tender farewell of the Prior and thought no more of him.

Time passed, and the Prior and his good sister were in despair. Meanwhile the accursed Magistrate continued to urge the marriage of his great booby of a son to the beautiful St Yves, who had been brought out of her convent for the purpose. She still loved her dear godson as much as she disliked the husband who was offered to her. The insult of having been put in a convent only served to increase her passion, and being ordered to marry the Magistrate's son was the last straw. Grief, tenderness, and horror were together driving her to distraction. Naturally, the affection felt by an elderly Prior and an aunt of forty-five could not compare with the love of a young girl in ingenuity and enterprise. Moreover, the novels she had secretly read in the convent had given her plenty of ideas.

The lovely St Yves remembered the letter which had been sent to Lower Brittany by one of the officers of the guard and which had been much discussed in the province. She made up her mind to go to Versailles herself and make inquiries; she would throw herself at the Minister's feet to obtain justice for her husband, if he should turn out to be in prison as they said. Something indefinable whispered to her that at Court nothing is refused to a pretty girl; but she little knew what it would cost her.

Making up her mind gave her some relief; she calmed down, and no longer repulsed her stupid suitor. She welcomed her detestable father-in-law, cajoled her brother, and spread happiness throughout the house. Then, on the day chosen for the ceremony, she set out secretly at four in the morning with her little wedding-presents and all that she had been able to gather together. She had made her plans so well that she was already more than ten leagues off when they entered her room towards midday. They were overwhelmed with surprise and consternation. The inquisitive Magistrate asked more questions in that one day than he had asked all the week, and the bridegroom was stupider than he had ever been before. The Abbé de St Yves, in a furious rage, decided to run after his sister, and the Magistrate and his son resolved to go with him. Thus it was that fate brought almost the whole canton of Lower Brittany to Paris.

The lovely St Yves was quite expecting them to follow her. As she rode along, she skilfully questioned postilions as to whether they had met a stout Abbé, an enormous Magistrate, and a young booby who were taking the Paris road. When she discovered, on the third day, that they were not far behind, she took a different route, and as much by good judgement as good luck contrived to reach Versailles while they were searching fruitlessly for her in Paris.

But what was she to do in Versailles? Young, attractive, without advisers or supporters, unknown, exposed to all possible dangers, how would she have the courage to search for an officer of the King's guard? She had the idea of approaching a Jesuit from one of the lower ranks of the Order, for there were grades to suit all levels of society. Just as the Lord has prescribed different forms of nourishment for the various species of animals, he has ordained that the King shall have his confessor, known to all who seek benefices as the head of the Gallican church. After him come the Princesses' confessors. Ministers do not have them: they are not so stupid. Then there are Jesuits for the common herd, and in particular, Jesuits for the ladies' maids, from whom their mistresses' secrets are learnt; a most important piece of work, this. The lovely St Yves approached one of the last category, who was called Father All-Things-to-All-Men. She confessed herself to him; she described her adventures, her present circumstances, and her dangerous situation, and she begged him to find her a lodging with some devout woman who would protect her against all temptations. Father All-to-All introduced her into the house of the King's Cupbearer, whose wife was one of his most trustworthy penitents. As soon as she was installed there, she made haste to gain the woman's confidence and friendship. She inquired about the Breton officer, and sent for him to come and see her. Having learned from him that her lover had been carried off after speaking to a First Secretary, she hurried to see this official, who was softened by the sight of a lovely woman, for it must be admitted that the Lord created women only for the purpose of taming men.

The penpusher's heart was melted, and he told her everything:

'Your lover has been in the Bastille for nearly a year, and without your intervention he would probably stay there for the rest of his life.'

At these words the soft-hearted young lady fell into a swoon. When she had come to, the clerk went on:

'I have no means of doing you a good turn; my whole power is limited to making occasional mischief. Take my advice; go and see Monsieur de St Pouange, who can do both good and evil. He's Monseigneur de Louvois' cousin and a favourite of his. The Minister has two familiars, Monsieur de St Pouange is one, and Madame de Belloy is the other, but she is not at Versailles at present. All you can do is to soften the heart of the patron I have told you about.'

Pursued by her brother and worshipping her beloved, the

lovely St Yves was in a pitiful state. She felt a spark of joy, but it was quenched with violent grief; hopes gave place to dismal apprehensions; she brushed her tears away, but as she did so, shed more; then, trembling and weak as she was, she plucked up her courage, and ran as fast as she could to see Monsieur de St Pouange.

CHAPTER 14

*

THE CHILD OF NATURE'S INTELLECTUAL
PROGRESS

THE Child of Nature made rapid progress in knowledge, and most of all in the study of man. The rapid development of his mind was almost as much due to his savage upbringing as to the spirit he was endowed with, for having been taught nothing during his childhood, he had not acquired any prejudices. Since his understanding had not been warped by error, it had retained its original rectitude. He saw things as they are, whereas the ideas we have been given in childhood compel us to see them in false lights all our lives.

'Your persecutors are abominable,' he told his friend Gordon. 'I pity you for being oppressed, but I also pity you for being a Jansenist. Every sect seems to me a rallying point for error. Tell me now, are there any sects in geometry?'

'No, my dear child,' said the worthy Gordon, with a sigh. 'All men are agreed about the truth when it can be proved. But they are all divided about hidden truths.'

'Or shall we say hidden untruths. If there had been one single truth hidden under that pile of arguments that has been minutely examined through so many centuries, it would surely have been discovered, and the world would have been in agreement on that point at least. If this truth were one that is necessary to us, as the sun is to the earth, it would shine forth as the sun does. It is an absurdity, nay, it is an insult to the human race, I will even say it is an outrage against the Infinite and the Supreme Being, to declare that there is a truth essential to man, and God has hidden it.'

Everything said by this ignorant young man, educated by

Nature, made a profound impression on the mind of the unfortunate old scholar.

'Can it be true,' he cried, 'that I have submitted myself to real misery, all for the sake of unreal fancies? I am much more certain of my misery than I am of efficacious grace. I have wasted days in reasoning about the liberty of God and the human race, but I have lost my own, and neither St Augustine nor St Prosper will rescue me from this abyss.'

The Child of Nature, yielding to his instinct, said at last: 'Will you allow me to speak to you freely and boldly? I have no great opinion of the wisdom of those who let themselves be persecuted for these vain scholastic disputes; but as for the persecutors, I think they are monsters.'

The two captives were thus in complete agreement about the injustice of their captivity.

'I am a hundred times more to be pitied than you are,' said the Child of Nature. 'I was born free as air. I lived for two things, my liberty and the object of my love, and they have been taken from me. We are both in chains, without knowing why or being able to ask. For twenty years I was a Huron; they are called savages because they take revenge on their enemies, but at least they have never oppressed their friends. I had hardly set foot in France before I shed my blood in her defence; I may even have saved a province; and as my reward I am shut up in a living tomb, where I would have died of rage without your company. Are there no laws in this country, that men are condemned without a hearing? It's not like that in England. It wasn't the English I should have been fighting.'

Thus, his increasing command of philosophy could not control a nature outraged in its basic rights, and left the way open to righteous anger.

His companion did not contradict him. Absence always intensifies unsatisfied love, and philosophy does not diminish it. The young man talked as often about his dear St Yves as about morality and metaphysics. The purer his feelings be-

came, the more he loved her. He read several new novels but
found few that depicted the state of his soul. He fancied that
his heart always went beyond what he read.

'Nearly all these authors have only wit and artifice,' he
remarked with a sigh.

And so the good Jansenist priest gradually became the confidant of his passion. Till then he had known nothing of
love except as a sin to be admitted at confession. He now
learnt to recognize it as a sentiment at once noble and tender,
one which can elevate the soul as well as soften it, and even
lead it into the paths of virtue on occasion. So here was the
greatest miracle of all, that a Huron should convert a
Jansenist.

CHAPTER 15

*

THE LOVELY ST YVES RESISTS CERTAIN
DELICATE PROPOSITIONS

THE lovely St Yves, who was even more devoted than her lover, went straight to see Monsieur de St Pouange, accompanied by the friend with whom she was lodging, their hoods pulled well down over their faces. The first thing she saw at the gate was her brother, the Abbé de St Yves, coming away. She was alarmed, but her pious friend reassured her:

'If someone has been speaking against you, that is all the more reason to speak for yourself. Remember that in this country the prosecutor is always believed, unless you hasten to answer his accusations. Besides, unless I am greatly mistaken, your presence will have more effect than your brother's words.'

It does not need much encouragement to make a passionate young woman fearless. Mademoiselle de St Yves appeared in audience, and drew everyone's attention by her youth, her charms, and her tender eyes moist with tears. For one moment all the Under-Secretary's toadies forgot the image of power to contemplate that of beauty. St Pouange took her into his office, where she spoke with such tenderness and grace that he was touched. She trembled, and he reassured her.

'Come back this evening,' he told her. 'Your affairs need consideration; we must discuss them at leisure. There is too much of a crowd here, and one has to hurry too quickly through the audiences. We must get to the bottom of this whole business of yours.' Then, after commending her beauty and her sentiments, he advised her to come back at seven o'clock that evening.

She did not fail, and returned at the appointed time with her devout friend, who remained in the antechamber studying Outreman's *Christian Pedagogy*, while St Pouange and the lovely St Yves occupied the inner office.

'Would you believe it, Mademoiselle?' he began. 'Your brother has been here demanding an order of summary imprisonment against you. I should really much prefer to issue one to send him packing to Lower Brittany.'

The lady sighed, and said:

'I see, Sir, how liberal you are in government offices with your imprisonment orders, since people come from the furthest parts of the kingdom begging for them as if they were pensions. I have no desire to take one out against my brother. I have much to complain of where he is concerned, but I respect human liberty; and that is what I ask, for a man I want to marry; a man to whom the King is indebted for the saving of a province, one who can serve him well, and who is the son of an officer killed in his service. What is he accused of? How can it be that he is treated so cruelly, without even a hearing?'

The Under-Secretary then showed her the letter from the Jesuit spy, and the one written by the treacherous Magistrate.

'Gracious Heaven!' she cried. 'Can there really be such monsters in the world? And am I, then, to be forced into marrying the ridiculous son of a man as ridiculous as he is wicked! And this is the sort of evidence on which the fate of our countrymen hangs!'

She fell on her knees and sobbed as she begged for the freedom of the brave man she adored. Her charms appeared at their greatest advantage while she was in this state. She was so lovely that St Pouange lost all shame, and hinted to her that she would succeed if only she began by giving him the first fruits of what she was reserving for her lover. Shocked and confused as she was by this request, Mademoiselle de St Yves pretended not to understand him; and he had to explain more clearly. He uttered first one indecent word, then a stronger one, followed by another more expressive still. He offered her not only the cancellation of the order against her lover, but compensation, money, honours, and establishments; the more he offered, the more anxious he became not to be refused.

Mademoiselle de St Yves burst into tears; she lay choked with sobs, half prostrate upon a sofa, hardly able to believe what she saw and heard. St Pouange for his part fell on his knees. He was not unattractive, and would have been able to prevail over a less dedicated heart; but Mademoiselle de St Yves adored her lover, and considered it a horrible crime to betray him in order to serve him. St Pouange redoubled his prayers and promises. At last his head was so completely turned that he told her that this was the only way she could release from prison the man in whom she took such a violent yet tender interest.

This strange conversation went on and on. The devout woman in the antechamber said to herself, as she read her *Christian Pedagogy*:

'Heavens! What can they have been doing in there for two hours? Monseigneur de St Pouange has never given such a long audience before! Perhaps he has refused this poor young girl everything, and that's why she's still pleading with him.'

At last her companion came out of the inner room utterly bewildered and unable to speak. She was meditating on the character of the great and their underlings, who so lightly sacrifice the freedom of men and the honour of women.

She said not a word on the way home; but when they got back to her friend's house, she burst out and told her all. The devout woman crossed herself and said:

'My dear friend, tomorrow we must consult our spiritual director, Father All-to-All. He has a great deal of influence on Monseigneur de St Pouange, for he is confessor to several servant-girls in his house. He is a pious and helpful man, who also advises ladies of quality. Put your faith in him; that is what I do, and it always turns out well. We poor women need a man to manage our affairs.'

'Very well, dear friend,' she replied. 'Tomorrow I will go and find Father All-to-All.'

CHAPTER 16

*

SHE CONSULTS A JESUIT

As soon as the lovely and disconsolate Mademoiselle de St Yves was closeted with her kind confessor, she confided to him that a powerful and sensual man was offering to procure the release of her future husband and demanding a high price for the service; she added that such infidelity was extremely repugnant to her, and if it was only a question of saving her own life she would sacrifice it gladly rather than agree to the proposal.

'What an abominable sinner!' said Father All-to-All. 'You had better tell me this wretch's name. Some Jansenist, I'll warrant. I shall denounce him to the Reverend Father de La Chaise, who will put him in the prison where your dear one is now lying.'

The poor girl was much embarrassed, and hesitated a long time before she finally resolved to name St Pouange.

'Monsieur de St Pouange!' exclaimed the Jesuit. 'But, daughter, that's quite another matter! He's a cousin of the greatest Minister we have ever had; he's a good man, who has our cause at heart, and a good Christian too. He cannot have had such a thought. You must have misunderstood him.'

'I understood him only too well, Father,' she sighed. 'I am lost whatever I do. I can choose only between misery and shame. Either my lover remains buried alive, or I make myself unfit to live. I cannot leave him to perish, nor can I save him.'

Father All-to-All tried to calm her with these soothing words:

'In the first place, daughter, never use that word "lover".

There is something worldly about it which might offend God. Say "my husband". For although he is not so yet, you regard him as such, and nothing could be more respectable.

'Secondly, although he is your husband in imagination and in prospect, he is not so in fact. Thus, you would not be committing adultery, a heinous sin which must be avoided as far as possible.

'Thirdly, actions are not entirely malicious or culpable when the intentions are pure, and nothing could be purer than the wish to rescue your husband.

'Fourthly, you have examples in the ancient records of Holy Church, which can miraculously guide your conduct. St Augustine reports that under the proconsulate of Septimius Acyndinus, in the year of our Lord, 340, a poor man who could not pay unto Caesar that which belonged to Caesar was condemned to death, quite justly, in spite of the maxim "Where there is nothing, the King loses his rights". It was a matter of a gold sovereign. Now the condemned man had a wife in whom God had combined beauty with prudence. A wealthy old man promised to give her a sovereign, and even more, on condition that he should commit this loathsome sin with her. The lady did not believe she was doing wrong in saving her husband's life, and St Augustine strongly approved of her generous submission. It is true that the wealthy old man deceived her, and perhaps her husband was hanged none the less; but she had done everything in her power to save him.

'You may be sure, daughter, that when a Jesuit quotes St Augustine to you, the saint must be absolutely right. I give you no advice. You are sensible, and presumably you will do your husband a service. Monsieur de St Pouange is a gentleman and will not let you down. That is all I can say to you. I will pray to God for you, and hope that everything will turn out to His greater glory.'

The lovely St Yves, no less terrified by the Jesuit's discourse than by the Under-Secretary's propositions, came back to her friend's house distraught. She was tempted to let death deliver her from the horror of having to choose between leaving the lover she adored in fearful captivity, and the shame of delivering him at the price of her most precious possession, which should belong only to the unfortunate lover.

CHAPTER 17

*

HER VIRTUE HER DOWNFALL

SHE begged her friend to put an end to her life; but the woman, no less indulgent than the Jesuit, was even more outspoken:

'Alas,' she sighed, 'delightful, polite, and famous as this court is, that is usually the way things happen nowadays. The humbler positions, as well as the larger prizes, nearly always depend upon someone paying the price which you are being asked to pay. Listen. You have moved me to confide in you, out of friendship. I tell you that if I had been as fastidious as you are, my husband would have had no chance of the minor post which is what he lives on. He is well aware of this, and far from being annoyed, he considers me his benefactress, and looks upon himself as owing everything to me. Do you really imagine that all who are in command in the provinces, or for that matter in the army, have earned their honours and their fortunes simply by their services? Many of them are in debt to their wives. Military honours are often bargained for, and the place has gone to the husband of the loveliest woman.

'Your position is even more interesting; for it is a question of restoring your lover to freedom, and then marrying him. It is a sacred duty which you are bound to carry out. Nobody has ever held it against the beauties and the fine ladies I have been talking about, and neither will you be considered anything but praiseworthy. It will be said that you only allowed yourself a little weakness because you had too much virtue.'

'Virtue indeed!' cried the lovely St Yves. 'What a sink of iniquity! What a country this is! How well I begin to know

170

men! A certain Father de La Chaise and a ridiculous Magistrate have put my lover in prison; my family persecute me, and the only help I can get in my tribulation leads to my dishonour. One Jesuit has ruined a fine young man, another wants to ruin me. There are nothing but pitfalls around me, and I have reached the very brink of misery. I must either kill myself or speak to the King: I will throw myself at his feet when he is on his way to Mass or the theatre.'

'You would never be allowed near enough,' her good friend told her, 'and if you did have the misfortune to say what is on your mind, Monseigneur de Louvois and the Reverend Father de La Chaise would have you buried in the depths of a convent for the rest of your days.'

While this excellent person was thus adding to the perplexities of that despairing soul and twisting the dagger in her heart, a messenger arrived from Monsieur de St Pouange with a letter and a beautiful pair of earrings. Mademoiselle de St Yves, in tears, refused to touch them; but her friend took charge of them.

As soon as the messenger had left, the confidential friend read the letter, in which the two ladies were invited to a little supper-party that evening. Mademoiselle de St Yves swore that nothing would make her go. The pious woman wanted her to try on the diamond earrings; but Mademoiselle de St Yves could not bear the sight of them, and fought against the idea all day long. At last, with no other thought in her mind than her lover, she was won over, and allowed herself to be led to the fatal supper.

Nothing had been able to persuade her to wear the earrings, but her friend brought them and put them on in spite of her, before they sat down to table. Mademoiselle de St Yves was in such a state of confusion and distress that she endured the torment; the master of the house took this for a very favourable sign. Towards the end of the meal, the confidant discreetly withdrew. Then the patron showed her a document revoking the order for imprisonment, another order for a considerable recompense, and a commission to take charge of a company. Nor was he sparing in promises.

'How much I should love you,' she said to him, with a sigh, 'if you did not want to be loved so much.'

At last, after a long resistance, and sobs, and cries, and tears, she was weakened by the struggle, and was so bewildered and exhausted that she had to give in. She had no other resource but a resolution to think only of the Child of Nature, while her tormentor relentlessly took advantage of the state to which he had reduced her.

*

CHAPTER 18

SHE DELIVERS HER LOVER AND A JANSENIST

AT daybreak she hurried to Paris, armed with the Minister's order. It is difficult to describe what she felt during the journey. Imagine a noble and virtuous woman, humiliated by her disgrace, yet intoxicated with tenderness, torn with remorse at having betrayed her lover, yet radiant with pleasure at the prospect of rescuing the man she adored. Her bitter experiences, her struggles, her success, all these were mingled in her reflexions. She was no longer the simple girl with her ideas restricted by her provincial upbringing. Love and misfortune had formed her character. Sentiment had developed as rapidly in her as had reason in the mind of her unfortunate lover. It is easier for girls to learn to feel than for men to learn to think. Her adventure had taught her more than four years in a convent.

She was very simply dressed, for the attire in which she had appeared before her fatal benefactor filled her with horror. She had left the diamond earrings for her friend without giving them another thought. In confusion and enchantment, overwhelmed with love for the Child of Nature and hatred of herself, at last she arrived at the door

Of that dread fortress, palace of revenge,
Which oft immures both crime and innocence.

When she was to alight from the carriage, her strength failed her, and she had to be supported as she entered with a beating heart, with flowing tears, and a brow perturbed. She was taken to the Governor; but when she tried to speak to him, her voice failed, and she could not utter more than a few words as she handed over her document. The Governor was fond of his prisoner, and glad that he should be freed. His heart was not hardened like those of some of his honourable colleagues for there are jailers who think only of the salary they earn by guarding their captives and build up a fortune on their riches; they make a living out of the wretchedness of others, while secretly feeling a horrible delight in their sufferings.

He had the prisoner brought to his room. On seeing each other, the two lovers fainted; but though it was some time before the lovely St Yves showed signs of life or movement, the other soon came to himself.

'This lady appears to be your wife,' said the Governor. 'You never told me you were married. It appears from my instructions that you owe your freedom to her generous efforts.'

'I am indeed unworthy to be his wife,' said the lovely St Yves, in a trembling voice, and fainted once more.

When she came to again, she was still trembling as she presented the order of recompense and the written promise of a company command. The Child of Nature was as much astonished as moved by all this; he awoke from one dream only to fall into another.

'Why have I been imprisoned here? How have you managed to get me out? Where are the monsters who thrust me into this pit? You are a divine being come down from Heaven to rescue me!'

Mademoiselle de St Yves hung her head; then as she glanced at her lover, she blushed, and a moment later, with her eyes full of tears, she looked away again. She told him at last all she knew and all she had suffered, except what she would have liked to hide for ever, and what anyone more worldly than the Child of Nature, anyone more familiar with court customs, would easily have guessed.

'Is it possible that a wretch like that Magistrate can have had the power to deprive me of my liberty? I can see now that it is the same with men as with the lowest animals; they are all capable of doing harm. But is it possible that a monk, a Jesuit who is the King's confessor, can have had as much to do with my misfortune as the Magistrate, without my having the least idea why this detestable rogue should persecute me? Did he make me out a Jansenist? And now, tell me, how did you come to remember me? I didn't deserve it; I was nothing but a savage in those days. And you undertook the journey to Versailles by yourself, without advice, without any help? You appeared, and my chains were broken! I see now that beauty and virtue have an invincible charm, which breaks down iron doors and softens hearts of steel!'

The word virtue provoked a fresh burst of sobbing from the lovely St Yves. She did not know how virtuous she was in the crime she reproached herself for.

Her lover continued thus: 'My angel, you have broken my chains. If somehow, I cannot imagine how, you have enough credit to get justice done in my case, can you not do the same for an old man who has been the first to teach me to think, as you have taught me to love? We have been drawn together by our common misfortunes, so that I love him as if he were my father. I cannot live without either of you.'

'What! You want me to go begging again to that man who . . . ?'

'Yes, I want to owe everything to you, and then I hope to owe nothing to anybody but you. Write to this powerful man, add one more to the blessings you have heaped on me, put the finishing touch to the miracles you have performed.'

She felt obliged to do what her lover asked. She tried to write, but her hand would not obey her. Three times she began the letter, three times she destroyed it. Eventually she managed to write it, and the two lovers left, after embracing the elderly martyr to efficacious grace.

Mademoiselle de St Yves was both elated and heartbroken as she led the way to the house where she knew her brother was staying. Her lover took an apartment in the same house.

Soon after their arrival, her protector sent her an order giving the worthy Gordon his freedom, and requested a meeting next day. Thus she came to learn that she had to pay with further dishonour for every honourable and generous action she performed. She was filled with loathing for this system of buying and selling the misfortune and the happiness of men. She gave her lover the order of release, and refused the rendezvous with a benefactor whom she could not see again without dying of grief and shame. The only thing that could make the Child of Nature tear himself away from her was to go and release his friend; he flew there. As he performed his duty, he reflected on what strange happenings occur in this world, and admired the courage and virtue of a young girl to whom two unfortunates owed more than their lives.

CHAPTER 19

*

THE CHILD OF NATURE, THE LOVELY ST YVES, AND THEIR RELATIVES ARE REUNITED

THE noble and admirable rebel was once more with her brother the Abbé de St Yves, the worthy Prior of the Mountain, and Mademoiselle de Kerkabon. Astonishment prevailed with all of them, but took different forms according to their situations and their feelings. The Abbé de St Yves wept at his sister's feet for the injuries he had done, and she pardoned him. The Prior and his tender sister were also in tears, but theirs were tears of joy. The horrid Magistrate and his unbearable son did not spoil this touching scene. They took to their heels at the first rumour that their enemy was at large, and fled to bury their stupidity and their fears in their own province.

The four actors left in this interesting scene were waiting with unsettled minds for the young man to come back with the friend he was liberating. The Abbé de St Yves hardly dared raise his eyes in front of his sister. The good Mademoiselle de Kerkabon exclaimed:

'So I shall be seeing my dear nephew again!'

'Yes, you will see him,' replied the charming St Yves. 'But he is no longer the same man. His bearing, his voice, his ideas, his mind, all are changed. He is now as worthy of respect as formerly he was raw and ingenuous. He will be the honour and consolation of your family. If only I could be the same in mine!'

'You are no longer the same either,' said the Prior. 'Whatever has happened to make so great an alteration in you?'

In the middle of this conversation, the Child of Nature arrived, leading his Jansenist by the hand. The scene then changed to something more unusual and moving. First came the tender embraces of the uncle and aunt. The Abbé de St Yves almost went down on his knees to the Child of Nature, who was so no longer. The two lovers exchanged glances which expressed all that they so keenly felt. The face of the one was seen to be beaming with satisfaction and gratitude; but in the other's melting, half-averted eyes there was a note of embarrassment. All were astonished that she should show even a trace of grief in so much joy.

Old Gordon endeared himself to all of them in the first few moments. He had shared the young prisoner's misfortunes, and that was a great claim on their affections. He owed his deliverance to the two lovers, and that alone reconciled him to love. The harshness of his former ideas had vanished from his heart, and he too had become a man, like the Huron. Each of them related his adventures before supper. The two Abbés and the aunt listened like children enthralled by a ghost story, and like grown persons, who are all, interested in tales of disaster.

'I am afraid,' said Gordon, 'there may easily be more than five hundred innocent people still bound by the same chains which Mademoiselle de St Yves has broken. Their miseries are unknown. Hands can be raised in plenty against the multitude of unhappy people, but there's seldom one to help them.'

This was only too true, and the reflexion increased his tenderness and his gratitude. Everything added to the glory of the lovely St Yves. All were amazed at the greatness of her spirit and the strength of her soul. Their admiration was mixed with the respect one cannot help feeling for someone who is believed to possess credit at court; but the Abbé de St Yves sometimes wondered how his sister had managed to obtain this credit so soon.

They were about to sit down to table at a very early hour, when who should appear but the good friend from Versailles, knowing nothing of what had been taking place. She arrived in a coach with six horses, and it is easy to guess whom the equipage belonged to.

She entered with the air of one who is an important person at court with urgent business to transact. After casually greeting the company, she drew the lovely St Yves aside.

'Why do you keep people waiting so long?' she asked. 'Follow me. Here are those diamonds you forgot.'

She could not say these words softly enough to prevent the Child of Nature hearing; he saw the diamonds. Her brother was amazed; the uncle and aunt showed only the astonishment of good honest people who had never seen such magnificence. The young man, whose mind had been improved by a year's reflexions, could not help making some in spite of himself, and for a moment showed his consternation. His lover noticed it, and a deathly pallor spread over her lovely face; a shudder seized her, and she could hardly keep on her feet.

'Oh, madam,' she cried to the evil genius. 'You have ruined me! You have given me my death!'

These words pierced the Child of Nature to the heart, but he had by now learnt to control himself. He did not refer to them, for fear of upsetting his mistress in front of her brother, but he went as pale as she.

Mademoiselle de St Yves, frantic at the sight of this change in her lover's face, dragged the woman out of the room into a little passage, where she threw the diamonds at her feet.

'You knew well enough that I was not seduced by these; but the man who gave them will never see me again.'

As the friend picked them up, Mademoiselle de St Yves added:

'He can have them back, or give them to you. Leave me, I beg you, don't make me feel so utterly ashamed of myself.'

So the emissary departed, without in the least understanding the agonies of remorse to which she had been a witness.

The lovely St Yves, in great distress, a prey to such physical turmoil that she had difficulty in breathing, was forced to take to her bed. But so as not to cause any alarm, she said nothing about her sufferings, and making weariness her excuse, she simply asked to be allowed to rest. Before she retired, she managed to reassure the company by all sorts of comforting and pleasing words, and her lover's feelings were inflamed by her glances.

Her absence from the supper table cast a shadow over it at first; but it was one of those shadows which give rise to fascinating and fruitful conversations superior to that frivolous gaiety people cultivate, which is usually no more than a tiresome noise.

Gordon gave a short account of the Jansenist and Molinist movements, and told how one party had persecuted the other, and how stubborn they both were in sticking to their opinions. The Child of Nature commented, and pitied those who are not content with all the discord already aroused by their interests, but find new ways of doing themselves harm for the sake of interests that are purely visionary, and absurdities that are utterly incomprehensible. While Gordon unfolded his story, his young friend made comments, and the rest of the party listened enlightened and entranced. They spoke of the extent of our misfortunes and the brevity of life. They observed that each profession has its own vice and its own danger attached to it, and that everyone, from prince to beggar, seems to cry out against nature. How is it that so many men turn persecutors, or parasites, or executioners of other men, and for such small reward? A man in power will give the order for the destruction of a family with utter indifference to all humane considerations; his mercenaries will carry it out with even more barbarous delight.

'In my youth,' said the worthy Gordon, 'I knew a relative of Marshal de Marillac, who was pursued through the length and breadth of his province just because of that famous but unfortunate man, and who finally hid in Paris under an assumed name. He was an old man of seventy-two, and his wife, who accompanied him, was about the same age. They had a dissolute son who at the age of fourteen had fled from his father's home to be a soldier; he had deserted, and abandoned himself to all manner of debauchery and wretchedness. Finally he assumed a different name and entered Cardinal Richelieu's service as one of his guards (for that priest had his armed guards, like Mazarin), where he acquired an officer's baton in that band of parasites. This adventurer was ordered to arrest the old man and his wife, and he did his duty with all the severity of one whose only desire was to please his master. As he led them away, he heard the two victims lamenting the long succession of hardships which had dogged them from the cradle. Among their greatest misfortunes they counted the profligacy and ruin of their son. He recognized them, but he took them to prison all the same, assuring them that His Eminence came before everyone else. His Eminence rewarded his zeal.

'I have seen one of Father de La Chaise's spies betray his own brother in the hope of getting a little benefice which he never received, and I saw him die, not of remorse, but of grief at having been cheated by the Jesuit.

'The role of confessor which I practised for so long has given me some knowledge of what goes on in families, and I have seen very few which were not plunged in bitterness while to outward appearance they wore a mask of happiness and seemed to be basking in joy. And I have always noticed that great afflictions are the result of our unbridled greed.'

'For my part,' rejoined the Child of Nature, 'I believe that an honest man with true and generous feelings can lead a happy life, and I expect to enjoy unalloyed bliss with my noble and lovely St Yves. For I flatter myself,' he added, addressing her brother with a friendly smile, 'that you will not refuse me as you did last year, and that I shall go to work in a more decent manner.' The Abbé was lavish with apologies for the past and with protestations of undying affection.

Uncle Kerkabon declared that this was the happiest day of

his life. The kind aunt was in ecstasy, and cried out through her tears:

'Didn't I tell you you would never be a sub-deacon? This sacrament is worth much more than the other. Would to God I had been honoured with it. But now I will be a mother to you.' Then they competed with each other in praising the gentle Mademoiselle de St Yves.

Her lover's heart was too full of the services she had rendered him, he loved her too much, to be deeply impressed by the incident of the diamonds. But he had only too clearly caught the words 'You have given me my death', and was secretly alarmed at them; his joy was spoilt even while their praise of his darling mistress still further increased his love. After a time they could speak of nothing else, and settled down to discuss the good fortune which these two lovers deserved. It was decided that they would all live together in Paris; and they made plans for their future grandeur and affluence, surrendering themselves to all those hopes that the least glimmer of happiness so easily arouses. But at the bottom of his heart the Child of Nature understood all too well the falsity of this illusion. He reread the promissory notes signed 'St Pouange', and the letters of appointment signed 'Louvois'; he heard these two men spoken of for what they were, and for what they were thought to be. Everyone discussed Ministers and the Ministry with that freedom of speech at meal times which in France is considered to be the most precious form of liberty to be tasted on earth.

'If I were King of France,' said the Child of Nature, 'this is what I should look for in a Minister for War. I would have a man of the highest birth, so that he could give orders to the nobility. I would insist on his having been himself an officer and having served in all the ranks, on his being at least a Lieutenant-General and worthy of being a Marshal of France. Surely he needs to have himself served in order to understand the details of the service? And would not the officers be far more ready to obey a man experienced in fighting, one who had shown his courage in the field as they had than a man from an office-stool who can only guess how a campaign should be conducted, however much intelligence he may have?

'I should not mind if my Minister were generous, although this might cause some embarrassment to the First Lord of the Treasury. I should like him to take his work easily, and even to be distinguished by the gaiety of spirit belonging to a man who can rise above events, which is what endears a man to the nation and makes all duties less painful.' He formed this notion of a Minister because he had always noticed that good humour is incompatible with cruelty. Monseigneur de Louvois would not perhaps have been satisfied with the Huron's notions, his merit was of a different kind.

But while they were at table, the unfortunate young woman's sickness took a sinister turn. Her blood was over-heated and a raging fever had set in. She was in agony, but she made no complaint, because she did not want to disturb the cheerfulness of the party. Her brother, knowing she was not asleep, went to her bedside and was taken aback at her condition. The others hastened to the scene with her lover at the head of them; he was of course the most alarmed and affected of them all, but he had learned to add discretion to the other gifts with which Nature had so liberally endowed him, and a ready sense of decorum came to his aid.

A local doctor was immediately summoned. He was one of those who visit their patients in a hurry, confuse the malady they have just seen with the one they are at present attending, and blindly practise a science which is uncertain and dangerous at best, even when conducted by a man of mature and healthy judgement. He made matters twice as bad by hastening to prescribe a remedy then fashionable. There are fashions even in medicine! This mania was too often the craze in Paris.

But even more dangerous than her doctor was the sadness of Mademoiselle de St Yves herself. Her soul was destroying her body. Her jostling thoughts carried into her veins a poison more dangerous than the most virulent fever.

CHAPTER 20

*

THE DEATH OF THE LOVELY ST YVES,
AND ITS CONSEQUENCES

ANOTHER doctor was called in. Instead of helping Nature and leaving her to work upon a young person all of whose organs were rallying to life, he busied himself only with opposing his fellow doctor. In two days the illness became mortal. The brain, supposedly the seat of the understanding, was attacked as violently as the heart, allegedly the seat of the passions.

'What incomprehensible mechanism is it that puts the organs of the body at the mercy of thought and feeling? How is it that one painful notion can upset the circulation of the blood and that this disturbance can in turn influence the understanding? Who can doubt the existence of an unknown liquid, more volatile than light, that in less than the twinkling of an eye invades all the channels of life, producing sensations, memory, sadness or joy, reason or madness? It can even recall horrors which were better forgotten, and make a thinking being into an object of admiration or a subject for pity and tears.'

These were the reflexions of the worthy Gordon. Natural – though unusual – as they were, they did nothing, for he was not one of those unhappy philosophers who force themselves to be unfeeling. He was as much moved by the fate of this young girl, as if he had been a father watching the lingering death of a beloved child. The Abbé de St Yves was in despair; the Prior and his sister shed torrents of tears. But who can describe the state of her lover? No language has the resources for such a climax of distress, for languages are far from perfect.

Mademoiselle de Kerkabon was almost unconscious, but she held the dying girl's head in her feeble arms, while her brother was on his knees at the foot of the bed. Her lover was holding her hand and bathing it with his tears, while sobs kept breaking from him. He called her his benefactress, his hope, his life, the other half of himself, his mistress, his wife. On hearing the word 'wife' she sighed, then looked at him with unutterable tenderness, and suddenly uttered a cry of horror; then, when a calmer moment of relief from the worst of her sufferings gave her opportunity and strength enough to express what was in her mind, she cried out:

'Your wife! Dearest one, that name, that happiness, that prize were not for me. I am dying, and deservedly. Lord of my heart! You whom I have sacrificed to infernal devils! All is over with me; I am punished! But you must live happily.'

Nobody could understand these tender yet terrible words, which filled their hearts with horror and compassion; but at last she had the courage to explain them.

A shudder of astonishment passed through all who were present; grief and pity were aroused at each word she uttered. They were all at one in detesting a man in power who had repaired a horrible injustice only by committing a crime, and had compelled that innocence that is most worthy of respect to be his accomplice.

'But why should you think yourself guilty?' cried her lover. 'No, indeed you are not. A crime must come from the heart, and yours is devoted to virtue, and to me.' He confirmed this statement with words which seemed to bring the lovely St Yves back to life. She was comforted and astonished to find that he still loved her. Old Gordon would certainly have condemned her in his Jansenist days; but he had learned wisdom, and now he admired her, and wept.

This scene of so much grief and fear, when every heart was filled with consternation at the danger to their beloved girl, was interrupted by the announcement of a messenger from the Court. Who could have sent him, and why had he come?

He had been sent by the King's confessor to the Prior of the Mountain; it was not Father de La Chaise who wrote, but Brother Vadbled, his valet – a very important man in those days. He it was who informed archbishops of the Reverend Father's wishes, who granted audiences and promised benefices, and who sometimes arranged for orders of imprisonment to be despatched. He wrote to the Abbé saying 'that His Reverence had been told of his nephew's adventures, that his imprisonment was just a mistake, that little accidents like these often happened and should be over-looked, and finally that the Prior was to come and present his nephew next day and bring the worthy Gordon with him, and that Brother Vadbled would introduce them to His Reverence and to Monseigneur de Louvois, who would have a word with them in the antechamber.'

He added that the story of the Child of Nature and his fight against the English had been told to the King, that the King would undoubtedly take notice of him as he strolled in the gallery, and might even give him a nod. The letter ended by expressing the hope that all the ladies of the Court would hasten to invite the Abbé's nephew to their levées, and that several would say 'Good-morning, Monsieur Child of Nature'; and that he would certainly be mentioned at the King's supper-table. The letter was signed, 'Your affectionate brother Jesuit, Vadbled'.

The letter was read aloud by the Prior. It put his nephew in a fury, but he contained his anger and said nothing to the messenger; then, turning to his companion in misfortune, he asked him what he thought of this way of addressing people. Said Gordon in reply:

'This is just treating men like monkeys! First they are whipped and then they are made to dance.'

Resuming his old character, which always returned at moments of great emotional stress, the Child of Nature tore the letter to pieces and threw them in the messenger's face.

'There's my answer,' he said.

His uncle was terrified; he thought he saw thunderbolts and twenty imprisonment orders descending upon him, and hurried off to write and excuse as best he could what he took to be a young man's fit of passion, which was really the flash of a great spirit.

But more grievous cares took charge of all their hearts. The lovely but unfortunate St Yves now felt her end approaching; she was quite composed, but with the terrifying composure of a nature so exhausted that it has no more strength to fight.

'My darling,' she said, in faltering tones. 'Death punishes me for my weakness, but I die with the consolation of knowing you are free. I adored you even as I betrayed you, and I adore you now as I bid you an eternal farewell.'

She made no vain attempt at steadiness; she had no notion of that wretched pride in making a few neighbours say that she died courageously. Who at the age of twenty could lose her lover, her life, and what is called honour, without regret and without heart-rending? She felt all the horror of her position, and she made others feel it by words and by those dying glances that have such power to speak. And then she wept like the others, in those brief intervals when she still had strength to weep.

Let others seek to praise the pompous deaths of those who face annihilation with insensibility. That is the fate of animals. We die like them only when age or sickness makes us their equals through the dullness of our senses. Whoever meets with great loss has great regrets; to stifle them is to carry vanity into the arms of death.

When the fatal moment came, all who stood around cried out, and wept. The Child of Nature fainted away. When the strong in spirit are tender-hearted their feelings are much more violent than other people's. The worthy Gordon knew him well enough to fear that when he came to he might take his life. All weapons were removed; when the unfortunate young man noticed it, he said to his relatives and to Gordon, without so much as a tear, a groan, or any sign of agitation:

'Do you really think that there is anyone on earth with the right or the power to stop me from taking my life?'

Gordon refrained from reciting to him those commonplaces which attempt to prove that we are not permitted to use our freewill by ceasing to exist when we are in a horrible predicament, that we must not leave the house when we can no longer live in it, and that man is on this earth like a soldier on duty. As though it were of any importance to the Supreme Being whether a collection of a few particles of matter is in one place rather than another! A man whose despair is firm and resolute disdains to listen to such ineffectual reasons, to which Cato replied merely by a dagger thrust.

The Child of Nature maintained a gloomy and terrible silence. His melancholy eyes, the trembling of his lips, the shudder that passed through his body, affected all who saw him with such a mixture of compassion and fear as to inhibit all faculties of the soul, and to exclude all speech except for a few half-formed words. The lady of the house and her family had hurried to the scene; his despair made them all tremble. They kept him in sight and watched all his movements. The icy body of the lovely St Yves had already been carried to a lower room far from the sight of her lover, whose eyes still seemed to seek her out though he was no longer in a state to perceive anything.

The corpse lay in state at the street door; two priests beside a font were absently reciting prayers; passers-by sprinkled odd drops of holy water on the bier, having nothing better to do; others were going on their way indifferently; the relatives were weeping; and the lover was near to destroying himself there. In the midst of this scene of death arrived St Pouange, with the lady from Versailles.

His momentary inclination, satisfied only once, had turned into love. The refusal of his favours had roused him. Father de La Chaise would never have thought of coming to this house; but St Pouange, with the image of the lovely St Yves always before his eyes, burning to assuage the passion which by a single indulgence had buried deep in his heart the sharpness of desire, did not hesitate to come in search of her whom he would perhaps not have cared to see three times if she had come to him of her own accord.

He alighted from his carriage. The first object that met his eye was an open coffin. He looked away, with the natural distaste of a man brought up on pleasures who considers he should be spared every sight which might lead him to contemplate human misery. He was starting to go upstairs, when the lady from Versailles, out of curiosity, asked who was to be buried. Mademoiselle de St Yves, she was told. At this name she grew pale and uttered a terrible cry; St Pouange turned round, surprised and grieved. The worthy Gordon was there, his eyes filled with tears. He broke off his mournful prayers to tell the courtier the whole story of the horrible catastrophe, and spoke to him with the authority that grief and virtue confer. St Pouange was not born wicked; the round of business and amusement had so much occupied him that he no longer recognized his better feelings; but he had not reached that moment of old age which normally hardens a Minister's heart. He listened to Gordon with lowered eyes, and wiped away a few tears, which he was surprised to shed; he knew repentance.

'I simply must,' said he, 'see this extraordinary man you speak of. I pity him almost as much as the innocent victim whose death I have caused.'

Gordon followed him to the room where the Prior, Mademoiselle Kerkabon, the Abbé de St Yves, and a few neighbours were restoring the young man, who had once more fallen into a swoon.

'I have been the cause of your unhappiness,' said the Under Secretary to him. 'I will spend my life repairing it!'

The Child of Nature's first idea was to kill him, and to kill himself afterwards. Nothing was more appropriate; but he had no arms about him, and he was closely watched.

St Pouange was not discouraged by rebuffs, or by the deserved reproaches, scorn, and horror which were heaped upon him: time softens all. Monseigneur de Louvois at last managed to make an excellent officer of the Child of Nature, who appeared under a different name in Paris and in the army, and was esteemed by all honest men for his fearlessness both in war and in philosophy.

He never mentioned this adventure without a groan, yet it was his consolation to talk about it. He cherished the memory of the tender-hearted St Yves to the end of his days. The Abbé de St Yves and the Prior each got a good benefice. The kind Mademoiselle de Kerkabon much preferred to see her nephew clad in his military honours than in a sub-deacon's robe. The lady from Versailles kept the diamond earrings, and received another beautiful present. Father All-to-All got boxes of chocolate, coffee, sugar candy, and crystallized fruits, with the *Meditations of the Reverend Father Croiset* and the *Flower of Sanctity* bound in morocco. The worthy Gordon lived in closest friendship with the Child of Nature till the end of his life; he got a benefice too, and he forgot all about Efficacious Grace and Concomitant Coincidence. He took as his motto: *Misfortune has its uses*. How many worthy people in the world have been in a position to say: *Misfortune is no use at all!*